DINOSAUR

H I D E O U T

DINOSAUR
H I D E O U T

JUDITH SILVERTHORNE

COTEAU BOOKS
WWW.COTEAUBOOKS.COM

Edited by Joanne Gerber.
Cover and text illustrations by Aries Cheung.
Cover and book design by Duncan Campbell.
Printed and bound in Canada at Transcontinental Printing.

National Library of Canada Cataloguing in Publication Data

Silverthorne, Judith, 1953-
Dinosaur hideout / Judith Silverthorne.

ISBN 1-55050-226-3

I. Title.
PS8587.I2763D56 2003   jC813'.54   C2003-910494-X
PZ7.S54DI 2003

10   9   8   7   6   5   4   3   2

COTEAU BOOKS

Fitzhenry & Whiteside
401-2206 Dewdney Ave
Regina, Saskatchewan
Canada   S4R 1H3

available in Canada and the US from:

195 Allstate Parkway
Markham, Ontario
Canada   L3R 4T8

The publisher gratefully acknowledges the financial assistance of the Saskatchewan Arts Board, the Canada Council for the Arts, including the Millennium Arts Fund, the Government of Canada through the Book Publishing Industry Development Program (BPIDP), and the City of Regina Arts Commission, for its publishing program.

The Canada Council for the Arts
Le Conseil des Arts du Canada

Canada

CITY OF REGINA

*This book is dedicated to my son, Aaron,
who shared his curiosity and his dinosaur books,*

and to my parents, Stan and Elaine Iles,

*and to my nieces "down-under" –
Tayla, Zara, & Shania*

CHAPTER ONE

The darkness of early morning enveloped Daniel as he slipped out the back door of the two-storey house. From the shadows of the snowy lane, he glanced back warily at his mother framed in the yellow glow of the kitchen window. He hoped she wouldn't notice him leaving. He didn't want to explain where he was headed.

At the moment, she had her back to the window and was sweeping her shoulder-length blonde hair into an elastic to keep it out of the way while she cleaned the kitchen. Daniel could see her determined face reflected in the mirror. She had the same dark brown eyes as him, but she was short and a little on the stocky side, while he looked more like his father – tall and slender.

Beyond his mom, he could see his plump six-month-old baby sister, Cheryl, in her high chair, playing with her pablum. Her blue eyes were probably sparkling with delight as she mushed it into the soft curls of her blonde hair. She loved to make a mess. As she plonked her spoon onto the floor, Mom bent to retrieve it. Daniel hurried past the large window. Mom would be kept busy preparing Cheryl for the babysitter before she left for her part-time nursing job in Climax, their nearest town. Mom had hoped to quit working after she had Cheryl, but they needed the money, so she still took as many hours as she could.

Daniel yanked his toque down on his head and quickened his pace. He'd have to hurry to get back home in time to do his morning chores before the school bus arrived, but he didn't care. He just *had* to check out his latest discovery. And that meant going to his special hideout. He might not have another chance till the weekend.

Shoving his mittened hands into his pockets, he plunged ahead. His boots squeaked and crunched across the snow-encrusted farmyard. He headed past the corrals where several horses milled about. Their snorts of recognition created puffs of fog in the brisk air. Gypsy whinnied at him.

Daniel walked over to his grey pinto mare and patted her soft warm neck. Gypsy nuzzled his toque and nibbled at his ear, messing his already unruly mass of dark brown hair even further. He slipped her a small carrot from his pocket, and gave her one more neck scratch before continuing on towards the pasture. Gypsy followed for a few steps, her hoofs crunching on the frozen ground, but Daniel shook his head.

"Not now, girl," he said, straightening his hat. Gypsy tossed her head with a snort and went back to the trough of grain.

To the east streaks of reddish gold emerged just over the horizon, casting the barn and granaries in shadowy outlines. Daniel passed a dark line of spruce and elm trees that encircled the buildings. Then he reached the open rolling landscape of the snow-covered pasture, all greyish white and billowy like endless clouds hanging low in the drab sky.

For all of his eleven years, Daniel had lived on the family farm, like his father, his grandparents, and great-grandparents before him. In the late 1800s, his great-grandfather Ezekiel Bringham had staked out the usual 160-acre quarter-section homestead, which lay in southwest Saskatchewan.

Daniel thought about the stories he'd heard, sitting on his grandfather's lap. How the family had managed to expand the farm by buying more land, but over the years it had dwindled again during the bad droughts, and other bouts of serious crop failure and low cattle prices. All that was left of the Bringham farm now was the home quarter with the house and outbuildings on it, one quarter for crops, and the quarter of pasture land that Daniel walked across. Not much for a prairie mixed-farm operation.

Tugging his toque farther down over his ears, he watched his breath emerge in the frosty air. Then he caught sight of his dog. He whistled.

"Dactyl, here boy."

A tail-wagging, slobbering golden retriever mutt greeted him from an adjacent bluff of trees. Daniel balanced himself on a hard ridge of snow as he murmured and patted his excited pet.

Dactyl had been given to him two years before by his parents, for his ninth birthday. He'd named the pup after one of his favourite Cretaceous period dinosaurs, because he'd dashed about and dive-bombed on his prey as if he were airborne like the flying reptile, the pterodactyl. The name was quickly shortened to Dactyl.

"All right, boy. All right." He grabbed the dog's collar and settled him back on the ground. He gave him one last scratch behind the ear, and then said, "We've got to hurry. Come on."

They trudged across the snow-covered ground, winding through several gullies and over gentle slopes. Dactyl occasionally disappeared around scrubby bush or over a dip, sniffing in search of an elusive rabbit. A slight breeze made the air brisk and tingly on Daniel's cheeks. In the distance, he heard the drone of a snowmobile. It was probably Doug Lindstrom, his best friend's dad, checking on his cattle.

As they walked, Daniel grabbed a stick from the ground and began throwing it for Dactyl to fetch. The dog made quick returns, slobbering and prancing about in front of him. It wasn't long before Daniel felt himself getting warmer. He loosened the ties at his neck and unzipped his jacket a few inches.

As the sun crept over the horizon behind him, he rounded the crest of a hill and dipped into a small side gully. He paused. The path snaked downward into a coulee – a deeply etched ravine and ancient riverbed, evidence that the land hadn't always been dry. Instead of following the steep track, he veered to the left and headed down to a snow-covered tangle of overgrown boughs and fallen logs.

More than a year earlier, he had discovered an abandoned cave lodged between the bases of the two hills. He'd dug the space deep enough for his own use, following a natural incision that had been created by spring runoff over the years. There were a few low bushes growing outside, but he'd hidden the entrance even more by dragging dead trees and branches across it.

Although it was well camouflaged, he quickly located the opening and began clearing a path through the drift of snow against the barricade. Then he crept under the branches and crawled inside the mouth of his hideout.

Instantly, he felt the cosy warmth of the shelter and smelled the damp earthy mustiness. Dactyl pushed his way in beside him and shook the snow off his furry coat, before dashing off to explore the interior. Daniel grimaced and brushed the moisture from his face with his mitts.

Then, careful to keep his head down, he crawled across the dirt floor. The cave was low around the edges, but once he reached the centre, he stood up easily. Next, he cleared the snow away from a football-sized opening overhead that let the emerging daylight filter in.

While Dactyl sniffed along the edges of the cavern, Daniel quickly scanned his collection of treasures. A bird's nest, a couple of deer antlers, several arrowheads, a rattlesnake skin, and some rusted coffee tins stuffed with special stones lined the floor along one side. Some low rock formations stood beside them, next to an old rolled-up sleeping bag.

He also had a collection of sticks and twine, and a pile of animal bones that he'd gathered from the pasture. Most of the things, he'd found in little digging and scavenging expeditions over the last two summers. He'd also tucked into a crevice a secret stash of emergency chocolate bars, some beef jerky, and a tattered paperback on dinosaurs that he used for reference. Right next to that, he'd placed his excavation tools: a small hammer, a chisel, a compass, and a fine paintbrush he used for brushing dirt from specimens.

He made his way over to a tree stump which he'd dragged into the middle of the cave. Through the opening above him, he could see that the sky was now frosty and bright with early morning light. He plunked himself down on the cold surface of the stump and reached for a plastic ice cream pail that housed his latest rock finds. Quickly, he dumped the contents onto the ground and began searching.

He chose a small rough stone and rubbed sand off one side with his mitts. Darn, that wasn't what he was looking for! He set it back down again and drew another and another, sifting through the pile on the ground. He was sure there had to be a special rock in his collection. He'd just read a description in one of his books on dinosaurs at home the night before, and something had clicked in his brain. He just had to find it!

Suddenly, he noticed a chunk of limestone near the bottom of the pile. He carefully wiped the oddly shaped stone free of dirt.

"Hey, there's some fossil prints on this one!" He spoke to Dactyl, but the dog ignored him and continued sniffing in a remote corner.

Could the fossil imprint in this rock be what he thought it was? Daniel brushed off more earth, feeling the excitement rise inside him. Handling it gently, he followed the indentations with his finger. He looked closer, and his eyes widened. Yes, this was definitely different from the others! It had criss-cross markings on it. He set the stone back on the ground carefully, threw off his mitts, then grabbed for his dinosaur book. He thumbed through the pages so fast that he almost ripped them.

All at once he sprang up and waved the rock at Dactyl.

"I knew it," he said. *"There were dinosaurs living here!* This is part of a receptaculites!"

He held the stone closer towards the light streaming

through the opening, turning it over and over, studying it from all angles. The criss-cross grooves looked just like the face of a ripe sunflower, for which the receptaculites were named. Now he had proof for the kids at school, who thought he was out to lunch with all his talk about dinosaurs on his farm. He knew that originally this particular spongelike organism must have come from the north Cambrian Shield. It would have been carried by glaciers and dumped in the south of the province. And this meant there *had* been dinosaur activity in his area – who knew what else was lying in wait for him to discover?

"Wow." He cupped the stone in his hands and stared down at it. His whole body tingled. He closed his eyes and imagined.

The bright blue of the sky was reflected in the shallow clear sea at his feet. As he touched the warm, sunlit water with his fingers, he peered down at the brightly coloured coral polyps and the golden-topped stromatolites formed on the bottom below. Crinoids with their orange fernlike flowers swayed. Just beyond them a huge dark red receptaculites bobbed in the soft current.

Then everything changed. The water became deeper and darker. He could just make out the faint outlines of sharks and rays swimming through the long clumps of seagrass. They made way for a large mosasaur that appeared from out of the depths. Rows of sharp teeth protruded ominously from its huge mouth.

Suddenly, an unexpected noise snapped Daniel back to the present. Dactyl's ears perked up, and at the same time Daniel heard the loud crunch of snow outside. A worn pair of boots and a rifle pointed into the doorway. He instinctively jumped to the side as Dactyl barked and rushed towards the entrance. A huge snarling hound met Dactyl head-on.

Startled, Daniel lunged for his dog's collar to haul him back from the attack. His heart pounded as his mind raced. How could he defend Dactyl and himself? Who was invading his hideout? Why? And what were they going to do with the gun?

"Who's in there?" demanded a gruff voice.

"I am! Don't shoot!" Daniel yelled back over the dogs' snarling. "I'm coming out. Call off your dog."

"Bear! Here, boy!" Someone yanked the brute out of the opening. "Heel."

Bear obeyed the stern voice of his master. But in a flash, Dactyl hurtled out after him, nipping at his heels. Daniel darted out and grasped Dactyl's collar firmly. He came face to face with a monstrous man dressed in a ragged parka. White hair bristled from under a worn toque, and he had a prickly beard. With gnarled fingers he clutched a rifle in one hand, while he gripped his straining dog in the other.

"What are you doing in there?" he demanded, coughing.

"Th-th-this is my special place," said Daniel, holding

onto Dactyl who struggled for another go at the intruding dog. Daniel shuffled his feet uneasily in the snow, still clutching the stone.

"I wasn't doing anything wrong," he said in a voice braver than he felt. This man had no right to be questioning him, but he wasn't going to argue with someone holding a rifle.

"Maybe, maybe not," he snapped. "You're Ed Bringham's son aren't you?"

Daniel stared, not saying a word.

"I've seen you around here," sputtered the old man, going into a coughing fit.

Daniel stared at the enormous figure hacking into a handkerchief. This must be the old hermit, Pederson, who lived nearby, on the next quarter to the south. Daniel had never seen him up close, but he'd heard stories about him from the kids at school. The guy was weird. *Really* wierd.

Once the old guy quit coughing, Daniel stood firm, but felt his legs quivering. What if the stories were true and Pederson was dangerous? Daniel glared as best he could, and with a slight tremble in his voice, declared, "Well, I have a right to be here. I *am* on my *own* property."

All at once, Dactyl yanked free of his hold and yipped in circles around Pederson and his immense mutt. Bear growled low in his throat, but stayed at his master's side.

"Well, see that's where you stay," rasped the old man

as he wiped his mouth and returned his handkerchief to his pocket.

Daniel dropped his eyes and found himself nervously fingering the rock in his left hand. Shivers ran up and down his spine.

"What's that?" asked Pederson.

"Just an old rock I found."

"Let's have a look." Pederson held out his arthritic hand.

Daniel hesitated, and then reluctantly handed over the rock. As Pederson took it, Daniel was sure he saw a sparkle of interest in the old man's eyes.

"A receptaculites. Lived here 'bout fourteen billion years ago."

"I knew it," Daniel blurted out. "I bet there were duckbills around here, too. Maybe even a whole Edmontosaurus with –" Abruptly, he quit talking, realizing he'd said too much.

The old man's face lit up for a few moments, and he seemed about to say something. But then his expression changed to a frozen glare. Daniel shuffled uneasily. Dactyl wiggled at his side, but stayed put. Pederson began coughing again, then spat on the ground and wiped his mouth with his hand.

"Where did you find it?" he demanded.

"Ah.... Well. Just around. You know. Out walking." Daniel avoided looking into Pederson's piercing eyes.

"Better not have been on my property."

Daniel stood defiantly. "No. I found it just a little ways over there." He pointed towards some hills to his left beyond his hideout.

Pederson's eyes widened. "You sure?"

"Yeah."

"So, how do you know what a receptaculites is? Suppose you learned that in school?" Pederson leaned in closer.

Daniel stood his ground. "No. Saw it in a book." He could hear the rasping in the old man's throat. "How do *you* know what it is?

"Saw it in a book."

They eyed one another for a few moments. Then Daniel extended his arm and opened his hand, glaring at Pederson. As the old man placed the fossil in his palm, his expression went blank and steely. Daniel stiffened, took a sharp breath, and slipped the rock into his pocket. Dactyl went rigid beside him, ready to charge.

All at once, Pederson doubled over with a fierce coughing fit, horrifying Daniel. He took a step towards the old man, about to touch his arm, but Pederson shrugged him off. Bear growled and Dactyl gave a sharp bark, but Daniel held his dog firm.

As his coughing subsided, Pederson loomed over Daniel and with a harsh look said, "See you keep away from my place – or you'll wish you had."

"Hey, no problem." Daniel backed away with his hands raised palms outward in front of his chest. As he stood watching Pederson stride away, he muttered, "Why would I want to go near your dumb place, anyway?"

He struggled to restrain Dactyl, who was barking wildly at the receding figures. When they vanished from view over a hill, he breathed a sigh of relief, and then kicked at some lumps of snow. Brushing off a log outside his hideout, he sat down. Dactyl padded over and put his head in his lap.

"Are you okay, boy?" he asked, examining the dog for injuries. "You look a little sore, but I think you're all right."

Daniel stroked Dactyl's head and thought about the encounter. He wasn't going to be taken by surprise again. Quickly, he rose and scrambled back into his cave. He shoved his hands into his mitts, then dragged out some twine, tin cans, and a number of old bones. He strung them up a few feet away from the entrance. Anyone approaching his hideout would trip on the string and the rattling would alert him. He hoped.

Suddenly, he noticed the sun higher above the horizon. It was getting late. He'd have to run to get home in time to do the chores and catch the school bus. Hastily, he tied the end of the rope to a bush. Then he gave a yell for Dactyl to follow as he scaled the side of the embankment. He could feel the cold winter air catch in the back of his throat as he hurried along. He'd better get back before his father missed him or he'd be in for big trouble! Lately Dad had been so stressed out about finances that anything might set him off.

Daniel would only have time to do the minimum feeding and watering of the stock, and that wasn't going to make Dad happy. He'd have to leave the rest for after school. Maybe he could do some extra cleaning then, so Dad wouldn't explode totally when he found how little had been done. He'd better turn his pace up a notch. He still had over half a kilometre to go!

CHAPTER TWO

J ust as Daniel reached the barnyard, he realized that he hadn't even had a chance to consider the importance of finding the receptaculites. The encounter with the weird old man and his dog had completely distracted him. But everything would have to wait for now. There were hungry cattle to be fed. And he'd better not be late for the school bus on top of everything else.

He opened one of the heavy barn doors just enough to squeeze himself through, and stepped into the huge old timber barn. Although the temperature was cool inside, it was many degrees warmer than being outdoors in the wind. The sweet smell of hay mixed with grain dust and manure filled his nostrils as he headed across the packed dirt floor towards the feed room.

Overhead in the hayloft, he could hear the little thumps of kittens' feet as they jumped off the straw bales onto the floor and came down to greet him. Marble, the orange calico mother cat, twined herself around his legs, until he stopped to give her a quick pet. The cows' movements made small rustling sounds in the straw bedding at their feet, as they chewed their cud and swished their tails at the odd docile fly that lingered from the autumn.

Grabbing a bucket off the hook, he began scooping grain into it as fast as he could. He quickly lugged pail after pail of oats to the two largest wooden-railed stalls, and dumped them into the feed troughs. That should keep the dozen cows and calves for the day. The animals pressed forward, jostling to be first at the trough as he approached. The kittens mewed and hissed as they darted across the barn, playfully chasing one another.

Daniel was distracted as he turned on the indoor water tap full blast and grabbed the hose. Water slopped onto his pants as he overfilled the water pail, but he ignored the freezing jolts on his legs. He had to hurry. The animals were counting on him. Dad already had enough to do with the outside chores and the milking. Dad didn't really have to keep on milking, but he was stubborn and wouldn't change his habits. Most of their neighbours just went to the grocery store and bought their milk and cream. Daniel could hear the tractor chugging outside as Dad hauled the stone boat full of manure to the pile behind the bins.

Just as he heaved the last pailful of water into the trough, he thought he heard the rattle of the school bus coming around the long curve before it stopped at his place. He dropped the metal bucket with a clang, and yanked the barn door open. The wind slammed it shut again as he sprinted across the yard.

Luckily, the sound was only a lumberyard delivery truck, probably Herb Milner passing by on his way to work in town. Daniel ran for the house and headed for a quick shower. He dressed quickly and ran downstairs, grabbing his parka and scooping up his backpack.

He'd barely stepped outside when he heard the rumbling of the school bus approaching his lane, then glimpsed bits of yellow through the profusion of trees lining the south side of the yard. As he ran, waving his arms to catch the attention of the bus driver, he realized he'd forgotten his lunch. He groaned and ran on. This was definitely not going to be one of his better days!

He took a deep breath and shifted his backpack as the bus wheezed and squeaked to a halt in front of him. He stepped on board, wondering what the rest of the week would bring.

As usual all the high school students and older kids were already on the bus. He was relieved to see Jed was also there, and slid into the seat beside his buddy. He and Jed Lindstrom had been friends since they were babies. Their birthdays were only a month apart, so they often celebrated together. The Bringhams and Lindstroms had farmed next to each other for several decades and were more like family than neighbours. Jed's three younger sisters actually treated Daniel like an older brother, teasing him whenever they could.

"Hey, Jedlock," Daniel poked his best friend, who'd made himself comfortable by taking off his parka and spreading his belongings on the seat, leaving little room for him.

"Mornin'," Jed answered, lifting his headphones off long enough to give Daniel the high-five, then pulling them back over his curly head. His long legs disappeared under the seat in front of them, evidence that he had sprouted up a few inches more than Daniel had in the last year. His shirt tails were half tucked into his jeans, a sloppy trait that Daniel didn't share.

Daniel nodded and smiled, then turned to look out the window. He barely heard the noisy chatter of his companions as the bus lumbered and jostled its way to town. He was thinking instead of the neat fossil he'd found earlier, and what that might mean. He'd have to figure out who it was safe to tell his secret to, besides Jed, of course, and who would help him find further evidence. Too bad he couldn't dig more until spring. The ground was frozen hard right now.

Suddenly, a nudge in his side from Brett Mortin, a grade eight kid sitting across the aisle, brought him back to the present.

"There's that crazy old coot, Pederson. Look." Brett pointed to the old man standing at the edge of a field ahead.

"So what?" said Daniel, stiffening and peering past the reflection of his face out the window.

In the distance, he could see a bulky figure standing beside a bend in the road, with a rifle propped upright in his crossed arms and his monstrous hound crouched beside him. Daniel felt a little quiver run up his spine as he remembered their encounter less than a half-hour earlier.

"He's probably looking for you Danny. He probably wants to see if you're nice and tender," Brett tormented him.

Daniel ignored Brett. When would the guy give up trying to persecute him?

Brett drew closer and breathed into his face. "Some night he'll come and get you out of your bed." Brett screwed up his face in a menacing gesture and stared at Daniel. "Then he'll throw you into a well until he's ready to eat you."

Daniel stared anxiously at Brett. He was more worried about being filled with buckshot if he set foot on the old guy's property, but what if the other stories were true? Maybe he'd just been lucky so far. He glanced back out the window, just as the bus rounded the curve where Pederson stood.

The old man's watery eyes and Daniel's met as the bus creaked past him. Daniel shivered and sank down into his seat. He didn't like to admit it, but he was terrified of the old coot, especially after his warning this morning. Now Pederson knew who he was.

"Geez, Brett. You've been watching too many horror

shows," Jed shook his head as he came to Daniel's defence.

Daniel shook off the panic and grinned tensely back at Brett as laughter erupted from the kids around them.

"Yeah, you're just being a jerk." Daniel shrugged Brett off.

"No, I'm not. It's true. He's probably looking for someone to bump off right now," insisted Brett, poking him in the side again. Then he lowered his voice, and said, "He murdered his wife, you know."

"Yeah, right," Daniel muttered. His heart did little flips as he remembered his fear when Pederson had pointed the gun in the doorway of his hideout earlier.

"Don't tell me you didn't hear the story?" said Wade, another grade eight boy.

At his side, Jed whispered, "Don't listen to him, Danny. He doesn't know anything." Aloud, he said, "Quit being such a dweeb, Brett. No one believes such a hokey story."

"What do you mean?" Wade persisted. "Everyone knows his wife died mysteriously, right?"

"Well, yeah. I guess I heard that," Daniel answered hesitantly. He could feel the fear rising again.

"Hey, it's true." Wade acted indignant.

"How do you know?"

"One day she was there and the next she was gone," declared Wade. "And nobody saw her ever again. He never took her to any hospital. He never took her to any doctor. He didn't have any funeral."

Brett nodded gravely beside him. "Nope, nothing. Nobody saw a thing."

"That's right, my uncle said so," chimed in Craig Nelwin from the seat behind them. His uncle owned land to the west of Pederson, and Craig and his brother spent a lot of time there. "He buried her right on his property."

"You're just saying that," said Daniel, wavering just a little. He'd ask Mom about it. Because she worked at the hospital and she'd know.

"There's no way," declared Jed, shaking his head. "He'd never get away with it."

"He's right," Wade butted in again. "I saw the wooden cross poking out of the ground when I was hunting for rabbits last summer."

"I saw it too," added Brett. "And he's always digging. He's probably buried other people on his place, too."

Wade leaned in closer, and whispered mischievously, "I even saw his jars of poison."

"No way," said Daniel and Jed in unison.

"Sure, they were all lined up on a shelf in his shack. I saw them through the window," said Wade.

"You actually saw them?" Daniel asked in amazement. He could feel his hands getting clammy.

"Sure," replied Wade nonchalantly.

Jed retorted, "Yeah, like you really snuck up to his place and peeked in."

"Did, too," Wade said defensively.

"He's telling the truth, " Craig said. "One time my brother even saw him hacking up bones on the kitchen table."

Daniel and Jed stared wide-eyed at one another and shivered. They sat quietly back in their seats.

Daniel had heard other stories about Pederson, too, since the old man had moved into the area a few years ago. He was sure going to stay out of his way and off his property. He'd managed to so far, finding no need to go there. There was plenty to do on their own property, and he hadn't had much time to explore in other directions. He shuddered. He'd never go *near* the place now. But Pederson knew where his hideout was!

"What's the matter?" Jed asked in a low voice beside him.

"I'll tell you later," Daniel whispered back.

But he didn't have the chance to talk to Jed all day. Not only had he forgotten his lunch, he'd also forgotten to do his math. He had to stay in at both recesses to catch up on the work. And during lunchtime, Jed and his sisters went to visit their grandmother in town, and Daniel sat alone in the lunchroom, paging through a dinosaur book he'd borrowed from the library. Whenever he glanced out the window, he could see it was snowing again.

By the time they were back on the school bus headed for home, all the other nosy kids sat around them and nothing could be told in private. Besides, Daniel was too hungry and miserable, and too worried about facing Dad with the undone chores from the morning. He still had all the stalls to clean, and that meant forking out the old straw and manure, and laying fresh straw bedding down on the floors in each of them.

"I'll call you later," he said as he shrugged into his parka and gathered his backpack and mitts.

"Sure, Danny," Jed nodded, as Daniel got up.

"Probably after supper," he called back over his shoulder, remembering all the chores he still had to catch up on.

From the side of the road, he saw Jed give him the thumbs-up signal as the bus continued on.

When he arrived home, Daniel stood listening outside the barn door for a moment, but couldn't hear anything except the rustling of the cattle. He breathed a sigh of relief and stepped inside. He hoped he had time to do some cleaning before Dad spotted him.

He hurried about, forking out the stalls, and throwing the old straw bedding onto the stone boat in the middle of the barn. He heard the wind howling outside the barn walls while he worked, and as usual the kittens scampered about play-fighting. He was feeding Gypsy when Dad strode in, dressed in his old barn parka over his denim coveralls and thick winter boots. He nodded curtly to Daniel as he grabbed a galvanized pail and the milking stool, then gave a customary slap to a cow to move her over to the side of the stall, so he could sit down next to her to start milking.

Whoa, he's really angry, thought Daniel, deciding it

might be better to work in the stalls away from him as soon as he was finished in this adjacent one. He brushed Gypsy's side with a grooming brush for a few minutes, then grabbed a pitchfork and quickly cleaned the manure out of a stall down at the end of the barn.

"So where were you this morning, Danny? Suppose you had your head stuck in one of those scientific books again?" Dad asked sarcastically.

"No, I was out for a walk with Dactyl," he answered, gritting his teeth. He'd never told his parents about his hideout and he didn't want to mention it now. He moved a couple of kittens out of his way and grabbed a square bale of hay. He broke it open and spread the straw on the floor of the stall, then stole a look at his father.

"Don't tell me it was those darn rocks again?" Dad didn't even look up, just kept his head pressed into the side of the cow he was milking. "You know Danny, you're responsible for doing your share of the chores before you go to school?"

"I know, I just forgot the time," Daniel replied quietly, setting the fork against the railing and bending down to pet Marble, who circled his legs.

Dad brushed off the excuse, turned, and stared at him. His eyes had become large and a deeper brown, so intense that Daniel took a step back. A strand of dark hair fell across Dad's forehead as it always did when he was agitated about something.

"You seem to be sidetracked these days. You need to

focus your attention back on the work here on the farm. Someday this will be yours." Then under his breath he added, "If the bank doesn't get it first." He waved his arm across the span of the barn. "Books and rocks, they have their place, but you don't need 'em. This is all you need, right here!"

"Dad, I know I didn't finish my chores, and I apologize, but this morning I found something really exciting. It proves –"

Suddenly, Dad stood up and waved an arm to cut him off.

"Look, Danny, I know you aren't all that keen on the farm right now, and maybe I wasn't either at your age. But what we do and how we live is important, especially now." Dad grabbed the pail of milk, ready to move on to the next cow.

Daniel ducked away, sighing. Why couldn't Dad even try to understand the importance of what *he* was doing? He looked back up at him; he was still in lecturing mode and ignoring Daniel's protests.

"You may find dinosaur stuff appealing for now, but you'll grow out of it. Besides, they're long gone, Danny. What's essential is what's here and now. Keep that in mind when you decide to go gallivanting again instead of doing your chores. Okay?" He looked at Daniel sternly.

"Okay, okay. I hear you," he said, then mumbled to himself, "loud and clear." He grabbed the pitchfork again and stalked off further down the length of the barn and across to the other side, as far away as he could get.

Why couldn't Dad understand how he felt? He'd been searching for dinosaurs for years and his own father hadn't even noticed! But then his Dad hardly ever noticed anything he was involved in, nor did he set foot in Daniel's bedroom. If he did, he'd see all the books, mobiles, and replicas he'd collected. Mom seemed sympathetic, but Dad had the final word on everything. Sometimes it seemed like Velcro joined them at the hip.

Daniel continued with his chores in silence. At last he filled the final pail of water, then struggled over to the trough with it. He was tired, and the water slopped over the edges as he walked. His hands ached with the cold. He hadn't eaten anything since breakfast, except an apple Jed had brought back for him from his grandmother's. It had been a terrible day. First Pederson, and now Dad yelling at him.

He struggled to lift the bucket to the trough, and finally hoisted it to the rim, managing to pour the water in without slopping too much over the edges or any more on himself. As he returned the empty pail to the feed room, relieved that he'd accomplished the task, Dactyl followed him, nosing into the corners. Then just as he set the pail down, Dad called from across the barn.

"Come on, Danny, let's go in for supper. This will do for tonight."

Daniel didn't hesitate for a moment. He followed Dad out of the barn in record time.

CHAPTER THREE

"**M**orning, Jedlock," Daniel seated himself eagerly beside his friend on the school bus the next day. "Now I can finally tell you my news. You're not going to believe it!" He reached into his pocket, but stopped short at the glum look on Jed's face.

"Mornin'," Jed said unhappily, staring out the window.

"What's up?" Daniel nudged him with sudden concern.

Jed spoke at last. "Did you hear about that oil company that wants to lease land around here?"

"Yeah. My dad was on the phone with all kinds of people last night, that's why I didn't get a chance to call you."

Jed turned to look at him. "Do you know what this could mean? We won't be able to cross any of the property and no more searching for dinosaur relics. They'll be digging up all over the place, levelling hills and putting in an access road. There'll be trucks and people everywhere. All that noise and stink."

Daniel shook his head and replied with assurance. "It won't happen to us. Sounded like my dad thought there were too many reasons not to do it."

"Oh, yeah?" Jed shook his head. "Some guy is coming out to see my parents tomorrow night. I overheard them say your parents were interested too."

"What? Get real, man!"

"This is *for real!*" Jed nodded.

"My parents can't be interested. My dad wouldn't give up the farm. It means everything to him. And we don't have enough land to do both. You must have heard wrong."

"No, they're definitely coming over to my place to listen to the spiel."

"Geez, that's awful."

Wade whirled around in his seat and confronted them. "What are you so worried about? It means big bucks for us all. My old man says he's going to be able to retire, if they lease. Then we can go south every winter." He crossed his arms smugly.

Jed guffawed. "Is that all you think about, Wade? Money? You're disgusting." He pushed Wade's arm off the back of the seat. "Besides, this is a private conversation, if you hadn't noticed."

"Fine, you little morons. Starve then, with that kind of attitude!" Wade bent his head over to Brett and they whispered something and laughed. A few moments later, they moved up the aisle to plague the McCaw twins.

Daniel lowered his voice, "This is terrible news. Especially with what I just found."

"What?" Jed asked.

Furtively, Daniel drew the rock from his pocket and showed him.

Jed fingered the relic. "What is it?"

"A receptaculites," Daniel answered.

"A what?" Jed asked.

"I just call it a taculite," said Daniel. "It's kind of like a coral or sponge, only really ancient."

"Wow," Jed shook his head in amazement, turning the rock over. "Do you know what this means? You've found the proof!"

"Yep. But I need more time to search." He took the rock back and slipped it in his pocket when he noticed Craig Nelwin trying to listen.

Jed kept his voice low. "Yeah, I heard my parents say that it would be more beneficial if they leased the land with your parents – you know the two west quarters beside each other."

"That means the quarter where my secret hideout is! I won't be able to go there anymore!"

"Yikes. That's bad for you!" Jed stared at Daniel.

"I have to do something. They'll ruin everything!" Daniel exclaimed in horror. "I know there have to be some dinosaurs on our land that no one has found yet. I can feel it! And I think this taculite proves it."

Jed responded. "But there may be one bright side. I heard they want Pederson's place, too. Could mean we'll be rid of that weird old guy. He gives me the creeps."

"Yeah, I'm going to stay clear of him." Daniel shuddered. Then he told Jed about the confrontation with Pederson the previous morning.

"Geez, I'd have been totally freaked out!"

"I was," Daniel admitted. "But now I'm curious to know what he's up to out there."

"Danny, you wouldn't go snooping around his place, would you?" Jed searched his face to see if he was serious.

"Nah, not worth the effort." He wasn't going to admit he was too scared to go.

"Whew. You'd better not. No telling what he could do."

Daniel could tell Jed was relieved, but he pretended to be fearless. "Don't tell me you believed Brett and Wade's story?"

"Not really, but there must be something to it." Jed peered at him.

"Yeah." Daniel said thoughtfully. "Sure wish I knew what!"

Daniel saw Jed jerk, alarmed, so he busied himself digging a dinosaur book out of his backpack. Jed seemed to relax, as they dropped the subject.

Early the next morning Daniel and Dad were doing chores together in the barn. The smell of dusty hay wafted into Daniel's nostrils as he swung a pitchfork full of straw into the calves' stall. He could hear the *squirsh, squirsh* of milk hitting the metal pail as Dad milked Lily, their prize Holstein.

"Jeez, why do I always have to help feed these stupid animals every day? There's never even one day's break. I never have time to do anything I want to do," Daniel grumbled as he struggled to lift a large bucket of oats into the feed trough. Dactyl ignored him. He poked in the straw looking for mice. The cattle ignored him, too, shuffling over to the feed trough.

This was Dad's life, thought Daniel as he headed to the feed room, not one he wanted for himself. Ed Bringham, the great farmer. Daniel had been sold on it, too, until he'd discovered paleontology, but now he didn't have any qualms about choosing something different. It wasn't his idea of fun to spend the rest of his life doing chores morning, noon, and night, seven days a week, like his father. It wouldn't even matter if they sold most of their cows, he sighed, if they had to lease the land: there'd probably still be one or two around, and the chores would carry on.

Dad was wrong about one thing, though. Daniel did want to keep the land, but he had other plans for it: do some archaeological exploration and search for dinosaur relics. He loved being able to walk in the pastures, too, and he wanted to know about everything that was part of the prairies: the plants, the birds, and the insects. Maybe even set up a nature refuge someday. There was a little bit of everything on their land. Sloughs, pasture, fields, trees, rocks, hills, and streams – all the ecosystems that Daniel would love to learn more about.

Harrumph. He hoisted another heavy pail towards the trough, scraping along the metal sides. Just as he was struggling to lift it to the trough, Dad finished milking and walked over.

"Here, let me help you with that."

Dad set down the pails of milk he'd been carrying and grabbed the bucket from Daniel. In one fell swoop, he hoisted it over the rim, and emptied the feed across the length of the trough, then stood back to watch the Holsteins chow down.

"Thanks, Dad," Daniel said, surprised by his sudden help.

Dad gave Daniel a tight grin, and tousled his hair.

All at once, Daniel felt the urge to blurt out part of his run-in with Pederson yesterday. He of course left out the part about his hideout and the reason he was there, and just zeroed in on the encounter. When he was finished, he wasn't surprised when Dad told him to avoid the man.

"He's not quite right in the head, Son. I'm sure I've told you that before," Dad said. "He's been living out there on his quarter all by himself for the past few years. He hardly talks to anyone, and you know we never see him in town, except once or twice a year. He's a loner, living off the land, hunting and fishing."

Lily mooed and shuffled against the railings and began chewing her cud.

"Have you ever been to his place?" Daniel asked, stooping to pet the cats crowding his legs.

"Once – he's got a nice quarter, good pasture. But he doesn't seem to use it for anything. I thought maybe I could make an arrangement with him. We sure could have used the extra pasture land to feed the cattle," said Dad, as he carried the pails of milk across to the separating room, and closed the door so the cats wouldn't get at them.

When he returned, he said, "Listen, Son, I don't want you going there, you hear?"

"I hear you, Dad, but what was it like?" Daniel gave the cats one last pet, then reached for a pail of oats to feed the horses.

"He seemed to know I was coming. Stood in the door and wouldn't let me in."

Daniel fed Gypsy, then Pepper, a large red roan. Then he set the empty pail down with a soft thud. Gypsy whinnied in appreciation of her breakfast. Daniel stroked her mane as she ate. Dad began forking clean straw into Pepper's stall. The stallion snorted approval.

"I only caught a glimpse of the inside of his place before he asked me to leave. It was pretty primitive. With old wooden chairs and such to sit on, and not much else."

Dad heaved another forkful of bedding into the stall.

"How come he lives like that, do you think?" asked Daniel, as he brushed Gypsy's flanks.

"Maybe just living by himself too long since his wife died, I guess," Dad replied, swinging another forkful.

"When did she die?"

"Four or five years ago, I think," Dad said.

"Did it happen in the hospital?" Daniel asked.

"I'm not sure," Dad answered. "You'd have to ask your mother. She'd probably know."

"Do you know how she died?" Daniel held his breath.

"Some mysterious illness. Kept getting worse. It was like her whole system was being slowly poisoned."

"Poisoned?" Daniel gasped and his heart jumped. "Did they ever find out what it was?"

"No...no one is really sure what happened. The..."

Brinng. Brinng. Dad's cellphone.

Daniel groaned inwardly. Now he wasn't going to find out anything more. He poked the pitchfork around in the straw, trying to look like he was busy as he listened to Dad's side of the conversation.

"Hi Doug." Dad listened intently for a few moments. "Sounds interesting. Yes, I planned to bring Libby along. Could be just what we need. Lord knows we have to do something."

Daniel slowed his pace even more, trying to understand what they were talking about, but he couldn't make much sense from Dad's end.

"Yeah, thanks. Might as well be prepared. Not looking forward to that either. Bye." Dad turned off his phone and closed it thoughtfully.

Daniel eyed him, holding back from asking about the call.

Dad slipped his cellphone back into his parka pocket, and reached for his fork again. "Maybe we should get extra bales down from the loft right now while we have some time. Doug Lindstrom just heard on the radio that there's a storm approaching sometime in the next couple of days. And I know the temperature's really supposed to drop tonight."

"Okay." Daniel sighed, stabbed the fork into the newly cut bale, and gave it a twist before he tossed a load into the next stall. Just what he really wanted to do! Lug heavy bails down from the loft.

As they hauled straw into the stalls, they worked together in silence. Daniel puffed at the exertion each time he threw a forkful, trying to keep up with Dad's quick easy swings.

After a while he asked, "How can Pederson afford to keep living on his place?"

Dad kept working as he answered. "I don't know how he pays his taxes Son, but I do know he probably owns that quarter and I doubt he ever borrowed any money to do any farming, so he wouldn't have outstanding loans to pay off. His father was one of the first homesteaders in the area."

"His father. How old is Pederson anyway?" Daniel

persisted, as he climbed onto the top railing and surveyed the barn.

"My guess would be in his seventies, but no one seems to know for sure. He left the area for a long time. I suppose he lives on his pension now." Dad set the pitchfork against the wall.

"Okay, enough questions. Time to get back to work."

He strode to the back of the barn. "We have to get these chores done so we can have an early supper. Your mother and I have a meeting to go to tonight at the Lindstroms."

"About the oil company?" Daniel persisted.

"Yes. You finish in here and I'll water the horses outside. We'll talk later." Dad left the barn abruptly, snapping the door behind him before Daniel had a chance to ask anything more.

At the supper table, Daniel squirmed in his seat, his butt slipping across the vinyl covering. Cheryl cooed in her high chair between him and Mom, playing with her mashed potatoes and gravy in her special bowl. Dad's head was bent over his plate, while Mom tried to feed Cheryl.

The kitchen was a large square, with the Formica table placed plunk in the middle and pale yellow cupboards stretching almost all the way around three sides. The only thing that had changed much since Daniel's grandmother's days were Mom's touches of homemade wall hangings, oven mitts, and curtains in a soft orange draping over the windows, giving a warm glow to the room. The oven had been on for a couple of hours, and loaves of fresh bread lay steaming on the countertop next to an apple crumble – his favourite dessert, right after Saskatoon berry pie.

Stabbing a sparerib from his chipped china plate – another kitchen relic left over from his grandmother's days – he looked over at Dad and asked, "You're not going to lease to those oil companies are you? It'll wreck the land, you know. They'll dig big holes everywhere, and ruin it. It won't be good for anything."

Dad winced and pushed his empty plate away. "We don't know yet what's going to happen, Danny. Not until we hear what the company people have to say. I'm all for keeping our land, but the southwest quarter wouldn't be too big of a loss. It isn't much good for anything, anyway. Doesn't even make great pasture land, unless we had more."

Daniel dropped his fork onto his plate with a clatter. "But there's lots of great things about it." He felt a sudden pounding in his head.

"Relax, Daniel," Mom soothed, wiping the baby's face and hands with a cloth. "We're just going to find out more about it. We're not going to make any rash decisions."

"Besides, Son, a few rocks and hills don't mean much unless you can turn them into a paying proposition." Dad pushed back his chair and stood up. "And raising cattle on them hasn't worked well enough so far either. There's never enough grazing land."

Daniel sat there with his mouth open as Dad headed towards the hall.

"We'd better go, Libby."

"Okay, I'll be ready in a jiffy," Mom said, wiping Cheryl's face and hands. Then she gave her a rattle to play with before she started clearing the food off the table.

Daniel crumpled his napkin and stared at Mom. "Money isn't all that important, you know."

"Your dad's just looking out for us in the best way he knows how." Mom gave him a sympathetic look.

"But, Mom, he doesn't understand what's maybe out there in those hills. It's way more important than money!" He rose from the table and began stacking the dishes, his usual after-supper chore.

"He's just trying to do whatever will help us stay on the farm. So keep that in mind." Mom looked at him sternly, and then softened. "We're only going to hear what these people have to say." Then she hugged him.

"Would you mind doing the dishes yourself tonight?" she asked, taking his baby sister from the high chair.

Daniel felt annoyed. "I can't come with you?"

"No, you have school tomorrow, and I don't know how late we'll be." Mom waited for his reply.

"Oh, all right." What was the point of arguing?

"Thanks, Sweetie."

He stood stiffly as she gave him another hug with her free arm. Cheryl gave him a big smile, and he took her while Mom went to the hall closet for their coats. He could already hear Dad starting the truck in the driveway. As Mom bundled up Cheryl and hurried outside, Daniel turned to the dishes with a heavy sigh.

After finishing, he helped himself to a large serving of apple crumble, and a Gatorade from the fridge. Then he wandered through the house with his snack. Everything was so still and quiet, except for the creaking of the maple floorboards as he headed through the dining room. He walked around the huge antique oak dining table, where Mom had arranged a bouquet of silk flowers in the centre, on a crocheted tablecloth. A matching china cabinet and sideboard sat together on one wall. Next to them hung a row of his school photos. He passed them and went through the double doorway into the adjoining living room. The television set sat on an angle in one corner.

For the next hour, he sprawled on the orange and yellow flowered couch, sipping Gatorade, while he watched his favourite *National Geographic* show. When it was over he carried the dishes back to the kitchen, being careful not to leave any evidence that he'd been eating in the forbidden living room. Then he went upstairs to his bedroom and scoured his books for more about receptaculites.

Every once in awhile, he'd get up and look out his

bedroom window to see if he could spot headlights from his parents' truck. At ten o'clock, he gave up on them and crawled into bed. He tossed and turned for what seemed like hours, until he finally fell into a deep sleep with vivid dreams.

He was crouched beside a large fern in a forest of cycads, dawn redwoods, sycamore, and cypress. The humid air made it hard to breathe. Odd screeches and sharp calls pierced the quiet. Sticky fronds scratched his face. As he pushed them aside, they felt cool, and smelled of moist grass. Through the dense foliage he saw a pale sun above the treetops.

Suddenly, a great crashing through the underbrush sent him squeezing further under the ferns. He tucked himself into a tight ball. A series of thundering booms shook the earth. His heart thumped hard in his throat – a massive triceratops rumbled through the bushes towards him. Its immense head with three long horns, framed by a huge shoulder plate, turned in his direction.

He held his breath and froze. He lay still and watched as the creature's giant elephantlike feet crashed down a few inches away. At last it pounded past him, shaking the ground. When it was out of sight, he gasped and sucked in deep gulps of air while his chest heaved. Slowly, the forest became quiet again, except for the weird screeching birdcalls.

He wiped the moisture from his face. Then he crawled out from beneath the fronds of his hiding place and carefully stood up. *A loud swooping sound came from somewhere behind him. He didn't budge or move a muscle as a large presence cast a huge shadow from overhead. Moments later the sky brightened again.*

When he dared to move, Daniel saw a flock of massive birdlike creatures soaring high above him. Their wings spanned ten metres at least – pterodactyls! In amazement, he stood there watching them. They were headed towards the mouth of a river he could see in the distance.

CHAPTER FOUR

With a start, Daniel awoke early the next morning. He lay there panting as he stared at the dinosaur replicas standing on his bookshelf. For a moment, he wasn't sure where he was, and then he realized he'd been dreaming. He'd always wanted to know what it would be like to live during the age of dinosaurs. Now he wasn't so sure! It had seemed so real! He shook the images away and flung back the thick quilt covers as if to throw off the fear and foreboding churning in the pit of his stomach.

Then he crept quietly down the stairs and poked his head in the kitchen doorway. He saw Dad poring over papers that lay strewn across the table. They were probably from the oil company. As he studied the pages, Dad's forehead creased and a look of despair washed over his face. Daniel's mother stood close beside him with her hands folded across her chest. She had a tight, worried look and bit her lower lip while she read. As Dad turned a page,

Mom leaned over to look closer and ran her fingers through her shoulder-length hair, twisting it nervously.

Daniel could hear the clock quietly ticking through the tense silence in the room, broken only when the refrigerator motor cut in. Here he was standing at the doorway of the most comforting room of the house, one where all things warm and cozy and nice happened in his family. And now everything he'd known all of his life was about to be torn apart and changed, and there didn't seem to be anything he could do to stop it from happening. There'd be no going back once a decision was made.

Mom reached out and touched Dad's shoulder gently with her fingers. "I'm not convinced that it's the right thing to do," she said in a voice trembling like it did whenever she was scared, which wasn't very often.

"Well, you know the situation we're in." Dad turned to look up at her.

"I know. But maybe there's another way to save the farm."

Dad sighed in exasperation. "Well, I haven't been able to think of one."

Daniel could stand it no more. He rushed into the kitchen.

"You aren't going to do it, are you? You said we'd discuss it."

His parents jumped and stared at him.

"Oh, good morning, Daniel," Mom said. "Yes, well, we are discussing it."

"But what about how *I* feel?" he asked.

Dad answered patiently, "Son, we know how you feel. We're taking that into consideration, and we'll talk about it with you later."

"Later, when? When you'd already made a decision?" Daniel couldn't contain his disappointment. "You can't do it!"

"Be reasonable, Son. This could be a great opportunity for us. It could help us get out of debt."

"No, it isn't. You're not looking at the whole picture." Daniel gazed from one to the other, injured. "You've decided, haven't you?"

"No, but your mother and I are seriously considering it, Daniel. It's a good proposition."

"They'll destroy the land," he protested. "They'll wreck all the possible dinosaur finds and, and...and it won't be any good for pasture for the cattle either."

"I know how you feel, Danny," said Dad. "I don't want to see the land damaged either, but the oil company said the disruption will be minimal."

"They're just saying that. It's not worth it, Dad," Daniel objected.

"Actually, it is. They're offering us a good price to lease the land. And we'll still be able to keep our home quarter and the northeast quarter, and farm alongside them."

Daniel pleaded, "And what about the important geological discoveries that could be made? They could benefit us all, too!"

"The only important geological discovery around here would be oil!" Dad retorted.

"But what about the T-rex discovery and the museum at Eastend? It could happen here, too."

"I don't see how. We need cash and we need it now. Times are tougher all the way around. There just isn't any other option for us."

"You don't understand." Daniel could feel himself getting hot all over. He clenched his hands at his sides.

Dad raised his voice and glowered at him, "No, *you* don't understand, Danny. It's either lease, or we lose our farm altogether. Do you want that to happen?"

Daniel felt like he would explode. He gritted his teeth defiantly and glared at Dad.

"Okay, everyone, let's just calm down," Mom interjected. "We're still in the discussion stage, and we can go over the details with you, too, Daniel."

She gave Dad a stern look. "Right now we all have chores to do and places to be, so let's talk about it later. Okay?" Then she turned her glare on Daniel.

"Daniel," she continued, making an effort to calm herself as she walked over and put her arm around him. "You must realize that ultimately your father and I will make the final decision. You'll have some input, but we'll have to do what's best for all of us."

"But Mom," Daniel wrenched himself free, "You can't do this. It's all wrong. I know it!" He rushed from the room.

As he grabbed his parka, stomped into his boots, and

plopped his toque on his head, he heard Cheryl's crying announcement that she was awake. Usually he liked to get her up in the mornings, but today he ignored her, knowing Mom would go to her. Instead, he reached for the snowmobile keys and headed out the back door. His parents had allowed him to drive the snow machine on his own for the last couple of years, so he knew they wouldn't stop him. He needed some distance right now.

Quickly, he pushed the Ski-Doo out of the shed. He jumped on it, turned the key, revved it up and propelled it around the buildings. As he roared out of the yard, he ignored Dactyl's barks from inside the barn. He didn't know how long he was going to be, and he didn't want to tire Dactyl out, or worse, have to call forever, looking for him.

He sped towards his hideout. His brain whirred. Lease the land? Not be able to go to his special place anymore? How could Mom and Dad even consider it? There could be all kinds of duckbills under these snowy hills! And what about other dinosaurs?

As he neared his hideout, he suddenly veered away. Just where were the boundaries of their property anyway? He hadn't been to the outer edges in ages. No need. He'd found everything he wanted right near his hideout. And why did the oil company want to lease this particular piece of land so badly?

After a few moments, he realized that was a no-brainer. If an oil company was interested, then for sure there were dinosaur remains. The two seemed to go hand in hand from what he knew. And there was no way he was going to let the earth destroyers anywhere near his special place. Not if he could possibly help it.

Wait! He must be near Pederson's property now. He slowed down and found a hollow. Then he cut the engine and sat there for a few minutes, gathering his courage. What could it hurt, if he took a little peek? He'd be careful, and the old man would never know!

He slid off the snowmobile and walked in the direction of Pederson's place, keeping a low profile. He slowed down even more as he moved in closer towards some low bushes that skirted the slope. As he crept along the line of shrubs, he looked down over the ridge. All he could see was a dilapidated cabin, more like a weather-beaten shack really, crammed into a gully as close as possible against the hillside. A sort of long, narrow lean-to jutted out from the main shack and butted into the hill.

As he tried to figure out what the purpose of the makeshift lean-to might be, Pederson emerged from it, carrying a pail of what looked like dirt. He dumped it onto a pile about twenty yards from the rustic cabin, and then disappeared back inside.

"Geez. What's he doing? I'm going in for a closer look."

Daniel eased himself down the side of the hill, keeping a careful watch in case Pederson reappeared. All was silent, except for his own scuffling footsteps in the snow.

He managed to sneak right up to the cabin, avoiding the debris scattered about the yard. He waited a moment, listening, then peered in the window. And gasped. Through the dimness of the interior, he could see all kinds of bones strewn out over a long wooden table on a back wall. He backed away a few steps, his heart hammering.

"Geez, maybe Brett and Wade were right! Wait until I tell Jed!" He squinted and thought about it. "Nah, it can't be."

He worked up his nerve to peer in again, hoping for a better look, while keeping an eye out for Pederson. But the place was too dark to see much of anything. He needed to be higher. He ducked back down again, and discovered an old metal pail nearby. As quietly as he could, he pried it out of the crusty snow. Then he turned it over, tamped it down a bit and stood on it. Cautiously he peeked back through the window.

He stared hard at the bones on the table. What were they? As he leaned in for a closer look, the pail tipped over and clanked onto its side, sending him sprawling with a loud thump against the cabin wall and then into a snow bank. Instantly, Bear charged snarling around the corner.

Daniel let out a yelp. "No Bear! Help! Get him off me. Help!"

All at once, Pederson appeared and yelled, "Heel, Bear! Heel."

He pulled his huge dog off Daniel, regaining control of him, then he grabbed Daniel by the scruff of the neck and half-dragged him away from the cabin.

"What in tarnation are you doing here, young man?" Pederson snarled as he yanked him along the ground.

"I didn't mean any harm, really. Let me go," Daniel struggled to his feet as Pederson set him upright again.

Suddenly, Pederson doubled over in a coughing fit and released him.

"I was just curious. Honest, I didn't mean any harm." He bent over and brushed himself off. That's when he spotted the little white cross sticking out of the snow halfway across the yard. He gulped.

Pederson wiped the spittle into a handkerchief.

"Do you know what I do to intruders?" he gasped out, breathing heavily.

"No, sir, I don't," Daniel said, although when he looked at the cross again, he had a good idea. Brett and Wade's comments came back to haunt him. He could feel himself shaking.

"Look, I didn't mean to intrude." Daniel had to try reasoning with him somehow. He felt tremors of fear shooting up his spine. Maybe the old guy did murder trespassers! He took a deep breath as he tried to think what to do.

"Maybe I could help you," he blurted out, holding his fear at bay and hoping to appease the old man at the same time. Besides, now he was even more curious to know what Pederson was doing. He was sure the bones he'd seen were too big to be human. Maybe they were from some huge animal?

"No. You get off my property right now. Go!" Pederson rasped out.

Daniel stood his ground. "Wait. I didn't mean to, but I saw the bones. On your table." Sudden realization dawned on him. "Are they from dinosaurs?"

Pederson stared fiercely at him, "Get. Now!"

"Please," Daniel's voice shook. "I want to know if you've found something important. I've been searching for evidence of dinosaurs for a long time. I know there's something special here. I just know it." Daniel swept his arm across the panorama of hills.

Pederson seemed to be wrestling with himself, weighing whether or not to speak. Daniel looked at him with pleading eyes.

"Please. It's important to me."

"Why? What makes you think I'd be collecting dinosaur bones? Does this look like a museum to you?" Pederson coughed into his handkerchief.

"My rock – the other day. You knew what it was. You're interested in paleontology, too, aren't you? That's why you're here."

"What do you know about paleontology?" Pederson went into another coughing fit.

Daniel started to move towards him to pat him on the back, but drew back when he saw the independent look in his eyes.

He tried to explain. "Enough to know that this has to be a prime place for dinosaurs. Enough to be sure that some amazing species are just waiting to be uncovered."

Pederson eyed him suspiciously. "So dinosaurs lived here once. Eons ago. That's no secret, given the makeup of the land."

"But that's what you're doing here, isn't it?" Daniel quizzed him. "Digging for dinosaurs?"

"Maybe, maybe not," the old man shied away from the question. "What are you expecting to find, young man?"

Daniel figured this was his chance to keep Pederson from doing anything bad to him, so he kept talking. Besides he felt tingly all over when he thought about his favourite topic. "I figure there's probably a whole dinosaur here. I mean, if they found almost a complete tyrannosaurus rex over by Eastend, why not here? We're only fifty kilometres or so away."

Daniel started clapping his mittened hands together to get the circulation going. He was beginning to feel cold, but he'd noticed the glint of interest in Pederson's eyes.

"What makes you so confident there's anything right here? On this land?" Pederson demanded.

"I've already found some fossils."

"What kind?"

Daniel noticed Pederson's increased curiosity. "Like what you saw the other day."

The old man shrugged, as if losing interest.

"And more," Daniel added shrewdly, wanting to keep his attention.

Pederson sized him up. He seemed to be making up his mind about something.

Daniel pleaded one more time. "Oh, come on. Tell me what you're doing. Please. I'm not going to say anything. My parents don't even know about my hideout. And my dad hates me mentioning anything about rocks and dinosaurs. All he's interested in is farming – cattle and crops."

"Is that right?" asked Pederson. He had another coughing fit that seemed to take his breath away.

Daniel shuffled uneasily, as he debated whether or not to confide in Pederson about his dilemma. Then he blurted out, "Did you know there's an oil company trying to lease land around here?"

"What?" Pederson stared hard at Daniel.

"Yeah," Daniel added confidently, "So that proves it, too. If there's oil, there are dinosaurs."

Pederson raised his eyes skyward, then said, "Not quite. You're kind of on the right track, but oil comes from a much earlier period than dinosaurs."

"Okay." Daniel thought for a moment. "But it seems wherever there is oil, it's also dinosaur country."

"Again partly true," Pederson nodded.

Then although he seemed about to comment further, Daniel plunged ahead. "That's bad news for me this time, though. The oil company wants the land where my hideout is, and I heard they probably want your land, too."

"Well, they won't get it," Pederson bristled. "Are you sure about this?"

"Sure as I'm standing here with you," Daniel regretted his choice of words, but blundered on. "My parents were at a meeting last night." He paused for effect. "Do you know what it could mean?"

Pederson nodded. "Of course I do. Can't let that happen." He muttered something to himself. Daniel thought he heard him say, "I'm too close."

"Too close to what? You can tell me. I promise I won't say anything," Daniel looked as sincere as he could.

Pederson hesitated, staring at him. Both of them shifted their feet, eyeing one another. Bear sat silently beside his master.

"Look, why would I tell anyone?" Daniel asked. "No one would believe me anyway. You're the only one that's ever seen my hideout. Not even my best friend, Jed, has been there."

Daniel crossed his fingers inside his mitts – true, Jed had never been there, but he did know the hideout existed.

"No one knows its location?" Pederson eyed Daniel.

"No one. I swear." Daniel looked up earnestly at the old man.

Pederson still hesitated, eyeing Daniel, as he coughed and spat.

Daniel hoped he sounded convincing. "Look, I'll tell you about some of my finds, if you like."

"Like what?"

Daniel stomped around as he talked, trying to get warm. "Like where I think there might be something big, like maybe a duck-billed dinosaur, maybe even an Edmontosaurus."

Pederson's interest was obviously piqued now. "Go on, I'm listening." He coughed again.

"Well, my theory is that because scientists have already found eggs from other duckbills just across the borders in Montana and Alberta, why not here? So far they've only found a few pieces of the Edmontosaurus in Saskatchewan. It would be cool to find a whole one, but even better to find their eggs," Daniel explained.

"And?"

Daniel looked at him incredulously, "And? Isn't that enough?"

"No." Pederson wheezed. "What's your proof?"

Daniel shifted anxiously. "Oh, all right. But you have to promise not to tell."

Pederson nodded.

"This fall, I found what I think might be a nest site."

"Really?" Pederson's eyes widened.

Daniel nodded and motioned with his head for Pederson to follow him. They climbed a little ways up a hill with Bear at their heels. Then Daniel pointed. "Just over there in the next gully – where our properties border. I found some coprolite there." Coprolite was fossilized dung. Proof that something had been out here, eons ago.

Pederson gasped in surprise, and then seemed to become even more agitated. He sputtered and coughed violently. Then he spat again, and held his chest.

Daniel looked on with alarm. It was a wonder the old guy hadn't choked to death. He must have pneumonia or something.

"Geez. Maybe you should do something about that cough?" Daniel could see the huge puffs of breath on the cold air as the fit finally subsided.

"It's nothing. Go on." Pederson commanded. He studied Daniel through watery eyes.

Daniel shook his head. "No, now it's your turn. You're digging up something, aren't you? What?"

Pederson looked away. He stood still for some moments staring mutely out at the landscape, before he turned a curious gaze back on Daniel. Then he seemed to reach some decision. He motioned to Daniel, turned and edged back down the hill toward his cabin. As he opened the rickety door, it threatened to fall off its hinges. He took no notice and went inside, stopping Bear, who wandered off to sniff out some tracks in the snow.

Daniel hesitated at the threshhold, reluctant to continue. What if the stories the kids on the bus had told were true? Was he walking into certain death? No one knew where he was. Should he leave while he could? Or stay and have his curiosity satisfied? Surely someone interested in paleontology wouldn't harm him? Or would he?

While he stood in the doorway trying to figure out what to do, Pederson turned to him in surprise. "Well, come in. Don't stand there all day. You're letting the heat out."

Daniel felt his face burning with embarrassment as Pederson turned away. Guess it's now or never, he thought and took a step forward. He stumbled inside the entryway and stopped short. The atmosphere was musty and earthy, but also warm. The place appeared to be a large one-room cabin, although it was hard to tell through the gloom.

When his eyes adjusted to the dimness, Daniel realized it was no wonder he'd tripped. The floor was nothing but old boards laid over mounds of packed dirt, that took a sudden dip towards the far wall, then disappeared under the makeshift cot. A woodstove sizzled in the middle of the room, its pipes contorting and rising out of the rafters. A small wooden hutch, which seemed to serve as a kitchen cupboard, leaned precariously against one wall.

As Pederson stoked the fire, Daniel shifted his weight. A clattering made him jump. He'd touched a chipped enamel dipper that hung on a nail on the wall, and sent it banging to the floor. Beside him, a metal pail full of water sat on a stool, and on the other side of the door stood a wood box full of firewood.

He bent quickly to pick up the dipper, realizing that Pederson didn't seem to have any running water. He peered around to see if there were any signs of electricity. There were some cords strung about, and one lamp by an old stuffed armchair.

Next he quickly checked out the weathered boards that served as shelves all along the length and height of one side wall. Stacks of books and magazines filled the bottom shelves. The top ones were lined with a myriad of jars, bottles, and tins in all shapes and sizes.

Daniel felt a clutch of fear. Maybe these were the ingredients for making poisons? Maybe Craig and Brett were right and Pederson planned to poison him. He gulped and eyed the recluse across the room. He had his back to Daniel and was removing his parka in between coughing fits.

He was probably harmless enough. He was an old man. Besides, he was sick. Daniel could probably outfight him and outrun him. And Bear was still outside so the odds were better. But what was in all those containers?

Daniel crept forward and examined the contents more closely. There were little labelled jars of dried plants, powders, crushed blossoms, dehydrated berries, and seeds in various shades of greens, browns, and yellows, all assembled neatly in alphabetical order. Just as he reached the last of the jars, Pederson poked him from behind.

Daniel jumped.

"Over here," the old man said and headed across the room.

Daniel took a deep breath and followed. The place was larger than it first appeared, he realized, as Pederson yanked on a chain and one side of the cabin flooded with light.

Daniel stopped short and gasped. Beneath the slanted ceiling of the shorter wall squatted a long rough-hewn table covered with dinosaur bones and various samples of fossil imprints! Even more than he'd glimpsed through the window.

"Wow! You're a real paleontologist aren't you?" Daniel stared at the old man.

Pederson nodded.

Daniel could hardly contain his excitement as he walked along the table, investigating the findings. He made sure not to touch anything, even though he really wanted to. Pederson watched him out of the corner of his eye.

"Wow! What are you doing out here? Are you with some museum?" asked Daniel.

"In a fashion."

Daniel looked over at Pederson, who had picked up a brush to remove dirt from a bone fragment at one end of the table. "What does that mean?" he asked.

"Used to be," the old man replied, not looking up.

Daniel looked at him curiously, waiting for an explanation. Pederson hesitated, then squinted at Daniel and proceeded.

"They scoffed at my theories. I believed, the same as you, that some dinosaurs, particularly those from the Cretaceous period, the hadrosaurs, or duckbills – as you suggested – actually existed and nested here. The museum administrators didn't want me wasting any more of their time or money on my searches."

Daniel became excited. "I know we're right!"

Pederson seemed to make up his mind about something, and all at once he motioned to follow him. He opened another door that Daniel hadn't noticed before. They entered a passageway that seemed to run into the side of the hill, and then rounded a curve and headed slightly downwards. Ah, the lean-to!

They came to a flat area where Pederson had obviously been digging. A strange whirring sound came from a few yards away. Several bare light bulbs hung overhead. As Pederson turned them on one by one, they cast patchy circles of light over the area. Daniel saw a small golden glow coming from the cracks around the door of a little tin stove in the far corner. Some old black stovepipe protruded from it and was kinked so that it lay on the dirt floor for several feet along the edge of a shallow pit. A fan attempted to spread the warm air. Finally, Pederson switched on the last light over a large cavity in the ground and stood aside to let Daniel see.

Daniel gazed in amazement at a huge ten metre oblong pit. It was about a metre deep in places and increased to two or three metres deep in others, where it framed massive brownish grey skeletal remains of some huge creature that seemed to have fallen in its tracks. One side of a giant curved rib cage was visible in the middle of the pit, surrounded by mounds of earth. Pieces of the bones were cracked or missing, and a massive skull with hundreds of teeth lay curved away from the main skeleton.

"Oh, geez!" Daniel whispered and turned to look at Pederson.

The old man nodded.

Daniel's voice was hushed. "You found one!"

He crouched down near one edge of the long pit and stared. "I knew there were dinosaurs around here! What is it?"

Pederson gave Daniel a slight smile.

"Not an Edmontosaurus?" Daniel squealed.

Pederson nodded with pride. "I believe so, yes."

Daniel knelt down beside the open pit and reached out to touch a long rib, then looked up at Pederson.

"Go ahead." Pederson nodded. His eyes seemed to be watering again.

Daniel gently touched the cold gritty surface of the fossilized bone, then ran his fingers partway up the length, as reverently as though it was a fragile newly hatched chick. The rib felt rough, with bits of dirt clinging to it, but he could see where Pederson must have cleaned other portions of the remains more thoroughly.

Daniel could hardly contain his excitement. "It's real! I can't believe it! I'm actually touching a real dinosaur."

As he stood up, he kept his eyes on the skeleton as if he were afraid it would disappear before his eyes. "We have to tell everyone!"

"No," Pederson barked out. "I want to finish first. I don't want people tromping on things, destroying evidence."

"I understand, but we have to tell someone. It's proof!"

"No! The answer is no!" Pederson snapped off the light and headed back up the tunnel. "I should never have let you see my dig."

Daniel followed, pleading, "No, wait. I won't say anything. I promise."

Pederson reached his outside door, flung it open and pointed for Daniel to leave. Daniel caught up and stepped out.

"Look, I'm sorry. And I won't leak it to anyone, okay?"

Pederson nodded. "See that you don't." He looked sternly at Daniel. "I'm counting on you to keep your word."

"I will." Daniel dropped his hands by his side and lowered his head. "I know how important it is to wait until you're ready. Thank you for showing me."

Pederson looked at Daniel's bowed head. "All right, then, be off with you, young man."

Daniel turned to leave.

"By the way," Pederson added, suddenly softening his tone.

Daniel paused and then looked back as the old man spoke again.

"Next time, knock."

Daniel grinned and Pederson gave an acknowledging grimace in return, before stomping back inside. As he headed back over the hill to his snowmobile, Daniel heard the old man coughing again. He started the machine and raced for home.

He hadn't done his chores on time for the second time in two days. Dad was going to be angry again – really angry. He'd been gone so long this time that Dad had no doubt almost finished the work without Daniel's help.

Then his thoughts whirred instead to his encounter with Pederson. Wouldn't Jed be surprised! He could hardly wait to tell him. But, of course, he couldn't tell him anything. He'd promised Pederson he'd keep his find a secret. That was going to be tough to do! Maybe if he just hinted and Jed figured it out, that would be okay? No. That was just as good as breaking his promise.

Maybe the warnings from Dad and stories from the kids on the bus weren't right after all. Pederson was a little strange, maybe even a little crazy, but he was no murderer. Daniel would keep his eye on him, and do a little more investigating. He'd sure like to talk to someone about it all. But that was just not possible yet. Instead, he'd read up all he could on the Edmontosaurus.

He cranked on the throttle and charged across the last stretch of flat pasture to the yard. As he rounded a bluff, the top of the barn came into view first. The old weathered two-storey timber structure stood as solid as the day his great-grandfather had built it. Of course, it had been repaired many times throughout the years. But it still served.

Just before entering the gate, he passed a long line of granaries and bins. Most of them were dilapidated and unused, including an old shed that he and his father were going to dismantle next summer. Right now, it hid the old automobile graveyard with its rusted out cars and trucks in various states of decay.

Daniel bypassed the barbwire corral fences that held most of their herd of cattle and their two horses. They'd trampled the snow into huge muddy areas adjacent to the barn.

Gypsy ignored him as he flew past a smaller empty pen fifty metres from the dugout. By now the surface of the rectangular watering hole was frozen over with a layer of ice several inches deep. Dad had to chisel out several openings every morning with an axe, so the cattle could have drinking water. Daniel was happy he didn't have that chore to do. He had enough facing him inside the barn.

Pulling the snowmobile up in front of the shed, he could see his mother's car warming up so she could leave for the hospital and take Cheryl to the sitters. He felt a twinge of guilt about not being there to play with his baby sister while Mom got ready for work, but this quickly dissolved when they came out of the house all bundled up and waved goodbye to him. Everything was under control. Now he'd better see what was happening in the barn. And face Dad.

CHAPTER FIVE

On the way home from school the next day, Daniel and Jed sat huddled together in the back seat of the school bus, speaking in low voices so the other kids wouldn't hear them.

"It's worse than I thought," Daniel complained. "My parents are actually considering the offer from the oil company."

"Mine, too," Jed responded. "They said if we don't do something quick we'll lose the farm. I can't even play hockey anymore, and my sisters have to give up figure skating. My parents said they couldn't afford the lessons or the gas to go into town. It's pretty tense around the house. My sisters were crying last night, and my parents are fighting all the time."

"Same here. Mine are arguing a bit, too," said Daniel. "I just wish there was something we could do to stop this from happening." Things sounded worse by the minute. Jed quit *hockey?* Though he'd never liked skating well enough himself to play, Daniel knew Jed loved hockey. He could be ferocious in a close game.

"We'd need a miracle." Jed stared out the window with a grim look on his face. "Sure is going to be a lousy Christmas this year."

As Jed studied the snow-covered hills they were passing, Daniel nervously bit his lower lip, wishing he could tell him about Pederson's find.

Almost under his breath, Jed spoke again. "We're probably going to have to move."

"No!" Daniel protested. "But where would you go?"

"Maybe to Calgary," Jed answered.

"That's terrible." Daniel's stomach did a tense flip-flop.

"My aunt and uncle live there. And my cousins. At least we'd know someone," Jed said quietly.

"But we'd never see each other again!" Daniel protested.

Jed stared more intently out the window; his lips formed a thin tight line like he was making every effort not to cry.

"Maybe there'll be some good news," Daniel attempted to distract Jed. "Maybe when the oil company does their testing, they won't find anything, so they'll go away."

Jed shook his head. "They'll still leave a mess."

"You're right. The damage would be done." Daniel bowed his head, just thinking about it.

"We'd be worse off than before," Jed added, turning back to Daniel. "I've heard that if they don't strike oil, they leave the farmers without anything, and then the land is useless, too."

Both boys sat in a dazed silence until the bus approached Daniel's stop. Daniel nudged his friend, and gathered his belongings quickly.

"See ya," Daniel said solemnly.

Jed nodded, but kept his head down as Daniel left.

As Daniel jumped off the school bus, a truck pulled out of his driveway. When he saw the oil company logo on the side of the vehicle, he hurried into the house as fast as he could.

Once inside the back porch, he threw off his boots and rushed into the kitchen. Dad was once again studying papers on the kitchen table. It was like déjà vu, yesterday all over again. Mom stood at the counter by the stove, forming meatballs and dropping them into the sizzling frying pan. Both jumped as Daniel came in and slammed his backpack on the floor.

"Daniel, what's the matter?" Mom asked, "You look all upset."

"I am. I saw the truck. You didn't sign that contract did you?" he demanded.

"Daniel! Drop the attitude this minute," Dad snapped.

"Sorry. But did you? I have to know."

"Not yet." Dad gathered the papers into a pile.

"We have a meeting with their representatives next Tuesday afternoon," explained Mom, turning her attention back to the stove.

"It'll ruin everything if you do." Daniel could hear his voice rising.

"Ruin what?" asked Dad.

"The land, for one thing. And – well, I can't say exactly," Daniel struggled for an explanation that wouldn't give away Mr. Pederson's secret. "But what if I told you that a really big scientific discovery could be made that would change everything for us. Maybe even make us enough money so we wouldn't have to lease the west quarter."

"And what might this amazing discovery be?" asked Dad with a touch of impatience. "I think I know what's on my own land."

"I can't...but...well...what if I told you I was sure there had to be something even bigger than at Eastend out there?"

"Yes, I could see that might be worth something. But somebody would have to find it. Some expert. That could take years and a lot of money. We're certainly not going to wait around for lightning to strike."

"But, Dad, what if I was positive?" He had to make him see.

"Well, you'd have to show me proof. Convince me somehow, I guess. Then I might reconsider, but even so..." Dad looked at him expectantly. "Well, can you prove it?"

Daniel wrestled with his conscience, until he thought he would burst. But in the end he knew he had to hold his tongue, because of the promise he'd made to Mr. Pederson. He sighed. "Well, not exactly. I mean, I can, but just not right now."

"We're back to that again," said Dad in exasperation, throwing his hands in the air.

"Daniel, we understand how important your scientific discoveries are to you, but..." Mom began.

"But you've got to understand our financial situation – we can't take vague speculations to the bank!" Dad finished the sentence for her in the stern voice that meant there would be no more discussion. Then he shook his head at Mom, and threw his hands into the air a second time. "We're doing it for his future, Libby. Doesn't he get that?"

Daniel felt his blood surging through his veins and into his head until it pounded. "Well, you can just keep your money and your farm. I don't want it," he cried. "If you had any idea –" He gripped the taculite fossil in his pocket.

"Sorry, Son, that's just not good enough." Dad shoved the documents to the side of the table as Mom began setting plates out for supper.

"Daniel, we have to go to the bank first, and discuss our situation with them," Mom explained calmly. "We don't even know what they'll let us do. Your dad has an appointment tomorrow to find out." She turned back to the stove.

"Now, how about washing up so you can help with

supper?" she asked gently, as she poured a can of mushroom soup into the pan. The aroma of simmering meatballs made Daniel's stomach rumble.

He whirled out of the room. At least he had until Tuesday to figure out a plan. He couldn't believe Dad's attitude! Just because he wasn't interested in archaeology, didn't mean he had to be so boneheaded.

He thought again of the table full of dinosaur relics at Pederson's, and the huge excavation site the old man was working on. In another instant, he pictured everything destroyed as a huge earthmover clawed at the land. He couldn't let that happen!

The next day after early morning chores, Daniel rode to town with Dad and Cheryl for their usual Saturday shopping trip. His mother had worked the night shift at the hospital and was joining them at the Linder Café for breakfast.

When they entered the small coffee shop, the aroma of just-brewed coffee and fresh-baked cinnamon buns enveloped them. The place was already filled with other customers, some of them their neighbours. They knew practically everyone, Daniel realized, greeting people as they made their way to the only available booth, at the back by the swinging kitchen doors.

Every time the waitress passed through the doors, a whiff of grilling bacon filled the air. Daniel saw Jed and his family and nodded across the room. Brett and Wade's families sat at one big table together, laughing and chatting without a care in the world.

Once they'd ordered, Mom played absentmindedly with her coffee spoon until Cheryl let out a squawk from her high chair and demanded it from her. Dad sat glumly, clicking a pen and making occasional scribbled notes on a scrap of paper on the table in front of him. From the short clips of conversation that Daniel heard buzzing about him, the major topic of the day was the oil company and what it meant to the community. His parents avoided the subject.

"I asked for more shifts," Mom said, then shook her head. "But there just aren't any. In fact, now that it's become a Wellness Centre instead of a fully operating hospital, they're cutting back even more on staff, so I'll probably lose some shifts that I already have."

Dad's expression reached another notch of desperation. Daniel turned his attention to Cheryl, keeping her quietly occupied with the dancing antics of a stuffed toy so he could listen.

"I could try going to the hospital at Shaunavon and see if they could use me there. Qualified nurses are hard to get in rural areas, especially out here," she offered.

"No, that's too far for you to drive every day."

Mom protested, "It's only forty-five minutes away!"

"Closer to an hour and if you times that by two..." Dad shook his head emphatically. "That's too much time out of the day spent driving, especially in the winter."

Her shoulders sagged.

"Maybe I'd better get over to the bank." Dad checked his watch. Mom leaned over to look, too.

"Too early," she said, patting his arm. "It's not open yet and you haven't even eaten."

Just then their food arrived. The chatter of conversations swirled about them, but the only sound at their table was the clanking of utensils on plates as they ate their $2.99 bacon and egg breakfast specials. Except for Cheryl, who played with a crust of toast and cooed at an elderly lady who used to own a dress shop in town. She made funny faces at Cheryl from across the aisle.

L ater, while Dad went for his appointment with the bald-headed bank manager, Daniel and his mother checked the specials at the local Co-op store and picked up a few groceries, before heading home in her car. Just a typical Saturday excursion, he pretended, as he watched the snow-covered farmyards flicking by through the car window. But his stomach flipped and contracted in alternate bouts, telling him otherwise.

D aniel sat hunched over a dinosaur book at the table when Dad returned from town later than expected. Mom had been holding lunch for over an hour when he finally came into the kitchen, and Cheryl was already down for her afternoon snooze. Dad seemed unusually subdued, not saying much as he sat down.

"So I saw the Schelova's have a new truck," Daniel said, in an attempt to break the silence. "What happened to their last one?"

Dad didn't respond.

"Mom? Did they have another accident?" He looked at her.

"I don't know, dear," she shrugged and glanced over at Dad.

"Do you know, Ed?"

Dad shook his head. Then he stared out into space.

"Looks like Misty is going to have kittens. Jed said this would be the last batch his folks will let her have."

Daniel was met with silence.

"How about if we take a couple?" he asked with an innocent look towards his parents, knowing they had plenty of cats. "We could use a few more to keep the mouse population down."

Mom and Dad kept eating, not saying a word for several more minutes. Finally, Mom seemed unable to stand the silence and asked what had happened at the bank.

"We'll talk about it later, Libby," was all Dad said.

Daniel eyed them anxiously, but neither brought up the subject again. This worried him, but he knew he'd have to be patient. Mom planned on sleeping for the afternoon and evening, because she had to work the night shift again, and Dad had to help one of the neighbours for a couple of hours. They both disappeared from the table abruptly.

This gave him just enough time to head back over to Pederson's to see more of his dig. He ran up to his room, grabbed his most comprehensive dinosaur resource book, and headed out. Maybe he could also persuade Pederson to speak up, so he could convince his parents not to lease the land.

As he put on his gloves and boarded the snowmobile, he called for Dactyl. His dog came on the run, yipping and tearing around in circles. Daniel started the Ski-Doo and headed slowly across the pasture. Dactyl loped at his side, only once in awhile venturing off around a bush or out of sight into a gully.

When Daniel arrived at Pederson's place, he decided to take him seriously. He knocked on the door. Then waited. He knocked again. Still no answer. He put his ear to the door, but all he could hear was Bear, barking from somewhere deep inside. He debated what to do. Finally, he rapped again, then opened the door and hollered.

"Mr. Pederson, are you here? Mr. Pederson?"

Everything was dark and quiet, except for Bear's continual barking. Daniel stepped inside, leaving Dactyl outside, and called to Pederson's huge mutt.

"Bear, here boy. Come on Bear."

Scrabble, scrabble. He could hear Bear coming up the passageway, breathing hard.

"Good boy, Bear," he said soothingly, stepping back somewhat in case the dog decided to take offence. But Bear whimpered as he approached Daniel. Daniel stroked him. "What's up, boy? Is something the matter?"

Bear paced back and forth towards the entrance of the passageway, as if indicating that he should follow. Carefully, Daniel skirted the long table with the array of fossils and bones, and followed him.

"Mr. Pederson? Are you here?" Daniel called as he walked along the dimly lit corridor. "Mr. Pederson?"

Suddenly, as he rounded a corner near the open dig, he heard a moan. It was Pederson, lying on the ground! He ran over and gently examined him for injuries. Then, seeing no blood, he shook his arm. He heard a rattling in the old man's throat. His face was pale and haggard, and his lips were turning blue. Daniel shook his shoulder a little harder.

Pederson stirred, gasping. His face was full of fear. Then he rasped out in a whisper, "My pills, on the table by the skull. The white ones."

Daniel rushed into the cabin and grabbed the bottle of pills, and then a dipper of water from the pail by the door, before racing back to Pederson. As he opened the pill container, he spilled some of the tiny tablets, but he didn't take time to pick them up. He had to get one in the old man's mouth. As he tried to give him some water, Pederson turned his head away.

"No water. Just need a minute," Pederson whispered

as he lay back with the pill under his tongue. He closed his eyes. When he began breathing easier, Daniel helped him sit up against the wall of the dirt passage.

"Thanks, lad." He opened his eyes for a moment. Then he shifted himself into a more comfortable position. "My heart medicine. Nitroglycerine."

Daniel began picking up the tiny white pills, but they were hard to find. Using a flashlight, he crawled on his hands and knees scouring the ground to make sure he had them all, brushing the dirt off them before placing them back in the vial.

"Sorry," he said to Pederson, as he handed him the container.

"No matter," the old man replied quietly, placing it in his shirt pocket. "Guess I overextended myself." He pointed to the excavation site.

Daniel walked over and took a look. Another section had been uncovered. He crouched down near one end and stared at the massive skeletal remains. All at once, he noticed something else half-hidden by the bottom of the rib cage. A nestlike indentation with what looked like fossilized fragments of shells! He stood up abruptly and faced Pederson.

"Is that...?"

Pederson nodded.

"You've actually found a nest," Daniel whispered.

"This is a fantastic discovery!"

"Look a little more closely," whispered Pederson.

Daniel dropped to his knees and crawled closer to the spot where the egg fragments lay embedded in the rock. There seemed to be almost a whole one. Gently he fingered the pieces. Then, moving a piece of cloth slightly, he uncovered the remains of a tiny skeleton. A whole baby Edmontosaurus!

Pederson and Daniel stared at one another, their eyes moistening.

"Do you know what this means?" Daniel finally gasped, in total awe.

Pederson nodded again. Daniel let out a whoop.

"Geez, this will make Saskatchewan famous in the paleontology world! First you found a whole Edmontosaurus – and now the nest! This'll be bigger than when they discovered the tyrannosaurus rex. Now you can tell everyone!"

"No!" Pederson rasped out, greatly agitated. "No one must know yet."

Bear barked and eyed Daniel, but stayed put, waiting for a command from his master.

"Take it easy, Mr. Pederson," Daniel said, going back over to his side to reassure him. "I'm not going to say anything." He patted his shoulder gently.

"Okay," Pederson said, still breathing heavily, but looking him intently in the eyes. "Just keep it that way until I say so. You have to promise."

"Promise," Daniel said, crossing his heart. "Scout's honour."

Pederson struggled to get to his feet, coughing. Bear paced beside him.

"Maybe I should get you to a doctor," Daniel said, as he grabbed his arm to steady him. "I have my snowmobile here. I could take you."

"No, I'll be fine, young man." He leaned a little against Daniel as they staggered back to the main room. Bear followed right behind protectively.

Daniel thought for another moment. "Wait! My mom's a nurse. I could take you home. She'd know how to help you," he offered as Pederson sank heavily onto the bed.

"It's just a touch of angina. I've had it for years," Pederson rasped out as Daniel covered him up with a couple of woollen blankets. "I just need to rest."

"Are you sure?" Daniel noticed that the old man's lips weren't so blue, but his face was still pale.

Pederson nodded and closed his eyes. Daniel stared down at him for a few minutes not speaking.

"Thanks, Daniel Bringham," Pederson said after awhile, patting his hand without opening his eyes.

"You're welcome, Mr. Pederson," Daniel said, tucking up the covers. "You sure you're going to be all right?"

"I'm sure. This has happened before. You'd best be going before your parents start looking for you."

Bear curled up at the bottom of the bed, his solemn

dark eyes glued on his sick master.

Daniel stared at Pederson for another few moments, watching to be sure he was breathing easier. He seemed to be. So, reluctantly, Daniel turned and left for home.

CHAPTER SIX

After he got back, Daniel spent most of the afternoon mulling over his books, studying everything he could about the Edmontosaurus. He already knew they had lived in the Cretaceous period in Saskatchewan, and were one of the first dinosaurs to be discovered on the prairies. But until now, no one had found a whole one, nor a skull, and certainly not a nest of eggs! And he'd seen it with his own eyes! Unbelievable! He could hardly wait to tell everyone.

Later that night after Daniel came back up to his bedroom, he heard his parents' raised voices. They must be deciding something important. They sounded upset. He crept out of bed and partway down the stairs. The dining room door had been left ajar. He could see Dad sitting at the table going through his bank statements and scribbling notes again. Mom stood against the china cabinet, her hands clenched at her sides.

"Well, it looks like we don't have much choice any-more, Libby. The bank won't give us another extension on our loan so we can try to lease more land from old Pederson or someone. In fact, they want us to pay off our line of credit right away." Dad ran his fingers through his short-cropped hair, greying around the edges.

"But why now all of a sudden?" demanded Mom as she walked over to the table and stared at Dad.

"Some new bank rules from head office. To do with the falling economy and the drought. They'll let us pay it off in two installments, but we have to make a payment next month and another in the spring."

"That still doesn't make sense," she objected, her face crumpling.

"It made sense the way the manager explained it. The bank is afraid of losing all their money because so many farmers didn't have good crops with the drought again this year, and most can't collect crop insurance. I don't agree with it, but the rules are the rules."

Mom paced behind Dad. "How can they be so inhuman?" she asked in a trembling voice.

"Guess we shouldn't have overextended ourselves buying that new tractor back when you were working full-time, before Cheryl.

"Oh, Ed. I can't believe we have to do anything before Christmas." Mom stopped, pulled down the bunched sleeves of her sweater, and crossed her arms over her chest.

"Well, it's either put the place up for sale now. Or lose it next year and end up with nothing," Dad's troubled voice echoed across the room.

Daniel couldn't believe what he was hearing. *Sell* it? He jumped to his feet and pounded down the stairs.

"We can't leave this place! We've always lived here," he argued desperately, clinging to the door frame. "Besides, you're always saying how important it is to stick at something no matter how tough the going gets."

Daniel's quick entry had startled his mother. "Oh, Daniel. We thought you were asleep. But now that you're up, you might as well hear. We were going to tell you tomorrow anyway."

He shuffled into the room and sat on the edge of a cushioned chair.

Dad cleared his throat. "I'm sorry, Son, there just doesn't seem to be any other way. We just don't own enough land to make the farm viable now that we've had two dry years in a row. There's no pasture for the cattle, and the bank won't give us any more time, or money for leasing land. We have nothing as collateral, nor any realistic way of making an income."

"What about selling the new tractor?"

"We don't own it to begin with, so that wouldn't help. Besides, our old one won't run anymore and we need something to use."

Dad stood up and pushed his chair back before continuing. "They said agreeing to the drilling lease wouldn't help much. We'd be better off bartering for extra pasture land or selling entirely." He began to pace the room as Mom had. "I'm sorry Danny. I know how you feel. But we may have no choice. Try to understand."

He came to a stop a few feet away from Daniel. He continued speaking as though mesmerized, all the while running his hands through his hair. "Even if we did have enough land, the crops have been so poor lately that we still might not be able to make a go of it. There just hasn't been enough rain for the last few years. As it is, we haven't even paid the taxes. And it goes without saying that if we lose the land, we can't keep the cattle or horses. We'd have nowhere to pasture them and nowhere to grow feed."

"What about Mom's nursing job? Doesn't that help?" Daniel asked. He could feel his body tingling as his heart thumped erratically.

"It keeps food on the table, but it's only part-time now and not enough." Then Dad added quietly, "The next payment is due at the end of next month. It'll wipe out just about everything we've saved. I'll see about finding a job off the farm, but we may well have to move."

Daniel stood there in disbelief, clenching his fists at his sides. His shoulders felt stiff and heavy, and his eyes stung as he looked from Dad to Mom.

"Move where?" he demanded. His stomach tightened and rolled in protest. "Not Swift Current or Moose Jaw!"

"We might have to go as far as Medicine Hat or Regina. Wherever we can make a living. It'll be a change, but we'll all get used to it." The worry lines deepened in Dad's face.

Daniel felt twinges of concern for Dad, but he couldn't help himself. "We can't go," he insisted. "Our family's been here for years. It's all I know." His voice shook. "What will happen to Dactyl and Gypsy? And Pepper, we've had him for years! And what about my friends? I'll never see them again."

"I know it's a shock right now, Danny boy, but if we have to leave, we'll find a good home for Gypsy and Pepper. Maybe you can keep Dactyl. And you'll certainly be able to visit your friends. And you'll make new ones."

"No, I don't ever want to leave this place. I won't go anywhere without Gypsy! There must be a way we can stay." Daniel grasped Dad's arm and pleaded. He felt his mouth tremble.

"We can't think of any, Son, and believe me, we've tried," Dad said softly, reaching to give him a hug.

Daniel's cheeks felt damp. "There must be something we can do," he croaked out, releasing himself from Dad's hold. Then he turned and headed out of the room.

His heart raced and his throat ached as he trudged up the stairs, entered his bedroom and closed the door quietly. This couldn't be happening! He took a few breaths, trying to calm himself. As he leaned against the door, he noticed the streak of moonlight that cut through the window and across the room, illuminating the full-length mirror on the opposite wall. He caught a sideways glimpse of himself, his face distraught and his dark hair standing on end where he'd swiped his hand through it several times.

Reflected above the door frame where he stood was an old framed print of craggy hills with a broken stream trickling at their base. It seemed askew. How fitting, he thought. His whole life was about to be screwed up. And he was definitely a mess, too.

Compelled by the distinct patterns of shadow and light in his room, he looked around over his unmade bed with its rumpled homemade quilt, and the clothes strewn across the floor. On his desk, his homework and dinosaur books lay scattered, one of the books held open with a banana peel. There was room for a computer, too, with an Internet hookup for his research, but that would never happen now.

Nearby were his shelves, lined with more dinosaur books and replicas. The mobile of planets and stars hung overhead, and next to it, barely visible in the dimness, were photos of nature hung alongside posters of atmospheric layers, the solar system, and a geological time chart.

Then his eyes lit on the scene through his window: the farmyard and the pasture beyond. The moonlight filtered softly over the yard. The tire swing dangled from the tree by the garage where he'd played for years. And the barbecue pit Dad had dug a few years back, filled with snow now, had been the site for the annual neighbourhood picnic.

He'd spent hours walking over the pasture with his

grandfather as he pointed out gopher holes, plants, nests, and footprints from foxes and deer. He'd helped his grandmother pick potato bugs off the huge garden near the dugout. He'd gone exploring on Gypsy's back more times than he could count. And what about his precious hideout? How many hours had he spent alone out there with Dactyl?

If he moved away, he wouldn't be able to do any of those things ever again. How would he spend his weekends or after-school times? His family would probably end up in some small cramped apartment like his great-aunt Helen's place in Regina, where he wouldn't know anyone. He shouldn't have complained about all the chores; now he'd have nothing to do to fill the hours.

Cheryl's fretful cries brought him back to the present with a jolt. Enough whining! He'd have to find a way to keep his parents from losing their land, that very land he was staring at. It meant everything to him.

When his breathing slowed again, he opened the door a crack and strained to hear his parents in the dining room below. Their voices were too quiet to distinguish and he didn't have the heart to hear any more. The faint smell of the roast chicken supper they'd had earlier wafted up and lingered in the hallway, reminding him that his normal, comfortable, predictable world was about to be turned upside down.

He closed the door softly and climbed into bed, then curled up in a ball and pulled the covers over his head. He lay there trying to calm himself for several minutes. Then he peeked over the bedding and looked again out the hoar-frosted window at the stars twinkling overhead in the cold night sky. He felt miserable.

A while later Mom came into his room and sat on the edge of his bed.

"Everything will work out all right. You'll see, Danny boy." She caressed the strands of his hair off his forehead with her hand. Somehow neither his parents' pet name for him, nor his mother's touch lessened the pain. "We can have a good life somewhere else, too, if we have to move," she said softly.

But he wasn't listening. In fact, he pretended to be asleep. When she turned at the doorway, he heard her add in a whisper almost to herself, "Guess it isn't going to be much of a Christmas for us this year."

His sleep was disturbed and filled with images. At one point he found it difficult to breathe.

He swam through murky water feeling the currents undulating around him. He floundered suddenly when he became aware of giant shapes all around him.. As a mosasaurus propelled its pointy head and huge body in his direction, he panicked. He struggled to right himself on the soft-bottomed sea, searching for a hiding place.

Just as the mosasaurus gained on him and opened its giant sharp-toothed mouth, he reached land and scrambled onto the *shore out of reach. He lay gasping on the marshy beach beside a dome-shaped rock. Suddenly, the rock moved and a huge turtle-like creature plodded into the sea.*

Daniel sat up quickly and looked around. The landscape merged and changed. It was his farmyard, only covered with lush birch and cypress forest, and beautiful plants in reds, yellows, and purples. The buildings were interspersed amongst the foliage. He decided to explore. As he wandered, small mammal-like creatures scurried through the underbrush, while overhead giant birds screeched.

When he rounded a tall bush, he stopped short. He gazed up at a huge Edmontosaurus nibbling on branches nearby. It stood almost fifteen metres long and was surrounded by several young. When the creature spied him, the balloonlike flaps by her nose inflated and she bellowed loud and long. The hard ridges on her back stiffened and her powerful tail swung.

All the youngsters bounded into the forest for cover, their tails straight out behind them as they scattered. Then the massive beast turned to confront Daniel, but he'd already dived into the bush and crawled through it to the other side. She lumbered around the thicket, and just as her three-toed hoofed foot was about to come down on him, he rolled away and curled up into a tight ball....

He woke up, sweating and cramped from holding himself taut. He lay panting and gulping for several minutes, then switched on the light and went to the bathroom for a glass of water. When he got back to his room, he sat on the edge of his bed, appreciating his familiar surroundings before taking a deep breath and crawling back under the covers again.

Once he'd snapped off the light, it took him some time to fall asleep. He saw three a.m. on his alarm clock and yawned groggily.

Daniel landed with a thud onto wet sand and when he rose, he was staring at little white crosses that punctured the ground sporadically over several metres. As his eyes shifted, more crosses would pop up. He stepped forward to take a closer look at one, but it vanished. In its place a huge nest of branches and ferns appeared, with a baby Edmontosaurus curled in the bottom. Everywhere Daniel looked, the crosses turned into baby dinosaurs.

All of a sudden, the sand shifted and gave way under his feet, trying to swallow him up. He flung his arms out, scrabbling and reaching for anything within his grasp as he sank. The dinosaurs changed back into white crosses, as he yanked on something soft and billowy nearby....

He awoke out of breath, clutching his pillow, with his bedclothes a total mess. But as he recalled the crosses in his dream changing into dinosaurs, he suddenly knew that the little white cross on Pederson's property was not marking his wife's gravesite. It was probably another excavation site! He'd take a closer look next time he was there. And he'd figure out a way of persuading Pederson to speak up. Then he could convince his parents of the importance of staying on their land.

CHAPTER SEVEN

Daniel finally woke up for good at seven a.m., bleary-eyed and groggy. The nightmares of the long night had left him feeling sluggish and distant, like he wasn't really part of his body.

He rose slowly, dressing and going through the motions of his daily routine. When he reached the kitchen his parents weren't speaking to one another, just sitting at the table sipping their coffee. He decided to do his chores before eating. Cheryl gurgled with pleasure when she caught sight of him, but he only gave her a quick tickle under the chin before heading to the door.

"Where are you going?" Mom called from the kitchen. "You haven't had breakfast yet."

"I'm not hungry," he said. "Maybe I'll have something later."

When he stepped outside, it was still dark and the wind whipped around him. He gasped in sharp breaths that made him feel more alive, but barely. As he walked towards the barn, Dactyl joined him, trotting along at his side. He seemed to sense Daniel's subdued mood.

Daniel's stomach felt knotted and his thoughts were a jumbled confusion. One minute he was afraid of losing the farm and of having to move. The next, he was excited at the possibilities of being able to doing something good with Pederson's phenomenal discovery.

If only he could convince the old man to speak about it, they might be able to join forces. Then they might kindle enough interest in the government and among the museum authorities to convince them to initiate a major excavation site and a tourist attraction. Sure, it was a dream, but it had happened over in Eastend with the unearthing of the tyrannosaurus rex, so why not at Climax? It could mean money for his family to stay on the farm. He didn't know how the details would work, but they'd figure it out somehow. Right after finishing chores and having breakfast, he'd go over to Pederson's and try to discuss it with him.

While Daniel ate breakfast, Jed phoned to see if he could come over for a little while. He'd have to be home by noon. Daniel agreed; he'd have to give up his plans of going to the old hermit's place, but he wanted to talk to his friend about the latest family crisis. Besides, Jed hardly ever had a chance to visit him. His family made him work really hard all the time, and he had hockey. Daniel was also eager to brainstorm about an official archaeology site. Somehow he'd have to find a way to tell Jed about his ideas without giving away Pederson's secret.

Daniel watched for Jed's arrival from the kitchen window, and as soon as he saw the Lindstroms' truck pull into the driveway, he hurried to the back door.

Jed smiled and gave him the high-five as he stepped indoors, then began unzipping his parka.

"Do you feel like doing some horseback riding?" Daniel asked, suddenly feeling the need to do something active.

"Sure, why not," Jed agreed. He zipped his parka back up.

As Daniel threw on his own parka and grabbed his boots, he called to Mom, who was upstairs bathing Cheryl.

"Mom? Jed's here and we're going riding," he called, pulling his toque onto his head.

"Fine," she answered, "Just don't be too long. I want you to help me later."

Daniel rolled his eyes at Jed. "Okay!"

The boys headed out the door before she could say anything more. They raced across the yard to the barn, their boots crunching loudly on the hard ridges of snow. The sun hung low in the sky, casting a yellowish haze over the farm, and the wind had died down.

As Daniel pushed the barn door open, he found Dad

inside, cleaning out the feed room.

"Hi, Mr. Bringham," Jed said as they walked past him, scrunching up their noses at the clouds of dust in the air.

"Hello, Jed," Dad nodded as he swept debris into a grain shovel. "What're you two boys up to?"

"Going riding," Jed answered for them, and then sneezed.

Daniel unhooked the saddles and harnesses from their posts and handed one set to Jed. They lugged them over to the horses. Gypsy whinnied and stamped her feet as they approached. Pepper shuffled in his stall.

"You take Pepper," Daniel said to Jed as he patted Gypsy. He murmured softly as he began saddling her.

Jed grinned. "Don't know why you named this horse Pepper. It sure doesn't have any spunk." He patted the horse's neck warmly, and said, "No offence Pepper, but your spry days are over."

Dad called over, "If you were as old as that horse and had worked as hard as he had, you wouldn't have any energy left either."

They chuckled together as they finished saddling their mounts, and led them out of the stalls. As the horses clopped along, the kittens scampered behind chasing one another.

"Looks like you picked a good time to ride," Dad said, going over to the barn door to open it for them. As he stood in the doorway, he said, "It's warming up some. Guess we're not getting that storm after all."

He patted Gypsy's rump as they passed by. "Have fun, boys!"

He closed the door behind them with a rattling bang as Daniel and Jed urged their horses across the yard towards the pasture. Once they cleared the last gate, Daniel made an instant decision and guided them towards his hideout. It was time he showed Jed his secret place. There might not be too many more opportunities.

Gypsy needed no extra urging; she seemed to know where they were headed. Jed followed behind on Pepper, sometimes riding beside Daniel, but the cold air caught in their throats and carrying on a conversation was hardly possible anyway. Daniel grinned at him, happy to forget his cares for a while.

Dactyl trotted beside them, occasionally weaving in and out of the scrubby bushes along the way, following tiny bird tracks. Little ice crystals glistened in the air, and the horses' hooves made sharp crunching noises on the packed snow. Ahead of them in the sky, they could see colourful sundogs stretching on either side of the sun.

"Where we headed?" Jed called out as they rounded a hill and started down a slope.

"It's a surprise," Daniel said, nudging Gypsy ahead of Pepper. Single file they rounded the last bend and came to the mound of branches and snow. Daniel slid from his horse, and tied her reins to a low bush just outside the entrance. Jed followed suit with Pepper.

Daniel watched Jed staring in surprise at the pile of

branches and the string of old bones and cans at the entrance of the hideout. Small animal footprints criss-crossed past the opening, but otherwise there were no signs of disturbance.

"What is this?" Jed asked, poking his foot curiously at a hole he spied in the debris. He rattled the string with the bones and cans. Daniel could almost hear the questions forming in his friend's mind.

"Come on," he invited, dropping to his knees under the string and moving a few branches out of the way. Luckily, there had only been a light snowfall since he'd last been here.

"It's my special hideout," he said proudly, and crawled inside.

"Wow! So this is it!" Jed exclaimed as he followed Daniel and caught his first glimpse of the dark interior.

Daniel stood up and cleared the overhead opening so they could see better. Jed gazed around the cave, stooping to touch things as Dactyl nosed about the crannies.

"Where'd you get this stuff?" he asked, holding up the deer antlers and staring at all the containers and articles lined up along the walls.

"Just found it all over the pasture," Daniel answered, shrugging. "Some stuff I brought from home." He pointed to the sleeping bag, the excavation tools, and the crevice where his dinosaur book was stashed.

Jed sat down on the stump and made himself comfortable. "How long have you had this place again?"

"Since a couple of summers ago," Daniel answered.

"No wonder you've kept it a secret. It's great!" Jed sounded amazed. "Can't believe you didn't bring me here sooner, though."

Daniel shrugged his shoulders apologetically. "Sorry, but a guy has to have some things totally private. Besides, I didn't find anything really spectacular until this taculite fossil." He pulled the rock out of his pocket and they examined it together.

"I suppose I'm not that great at keeping secrets, either," Jed admitted.

"You're telling me," said Daniel, shaking his head and recalling times when Jed had let it slip about some of their plans. "We'd have made it to town on our bikes to see that Arnold Schwarzenegger movie that time, if you hadn't told your sisters what we were up to."

"Heh, that was three years ago," Jed said, laughing. "Besides our parents would have grounded us for a week if we'd actually made it."

"The weekend was bad enough!" Daniel chided him.

"I've learned my lesson."

"Okay, then, so make sure you keep this place quiet!" Daniel insisted.

"Not a problem," Jed gave Daniel a thumbs-up sign.

Daniel pulled over the rolled-up sleeping bag and sat on it beside Jed. He might as well get right to discussing his ideas.

"Do you remember our class trip to the T-rex

Discovery Centre at Eastend?" Daniel figured this was the best way to start. Several classes had travelled on a bus to the centre, which was located outside the town and built into the side of a hill. The place was huge, with all kinds of paleontological activities to do and plenty to see in the viewing gallery. They'd even gone to an active dig site.

"Sure! That was way cool," said Jed. "That fossil-finding stuff was really neat."

"Yeah!" Daniel agreed. "Well, I think we could do something like that here."

"Get real," said Jed, staring at his friend in surprise. "We don't have anything special like the T-rex to show off."

"But what if we did? Wouldn't that be great?"

"Sure, but first we have to find something fantastic, then we have to convince someone to build a place." Jed eyed Daniel curiously. "Do you know something I don't know?"

Daniel shook his head, but he kept his eyes lowered. Keeping big secrets from his friend was going to be harder than he thought. In comparison, not telling him about the location of the hideout was easy, because there really wasn't much to tell. But with Pederson's discovery there was so much he wanted to discuss with Jed. It could change their whole lives.

"You're not basing this on finding the taculite, are you?" Jed asked in a mocking tone.

"No," Daniel answered. "But I do think it shows there could be possibilities."

Jed's eyes narrowed suspiciously. "You're keeping something from me, aren't you?"

"Not really," Daniel denied, squirming. "If there was something I could tell you, I would," he said truthfully.

Jed shrugged. "Okay, but unless you unearthed something really major, they'd never build a huge place like that here. Eastend isn't that far away."

Daniel's body tingled all over. Pederson *had* unearthed something major! "So, maybe they'd have something smaller here, like a research outstation or a town museum. But we could charge people to come," he waved his arms about, excited.

Jed grinned. "Yeah, and people could go on hiking trails, and excavation sites, too. That would be fun!"

"And field camping trips, just like at the Royal Tyrrell Museum in Alberta, or the T-rex Discovery Centre," Daniel added, envisioning busloads of people arriving in their driveway. "My mom could serve coffee and donuts, or maybe sandwiches. Then she wouldn't have to drive into town to work all the time."

"Speaking of food," Jed interrupted. "I'm hungry. I'd better get home soon for dinner."

"Can't you stay?"

"No, I promised," Jed shook his head. "My aunt and uncle are coming. And my cousins."

"Not the aunt and uncle from Calgary? Where you might have to move?"

Jed nodded sadly.

Daniel sat glumly for a moment, and then he grinned at his friend, who was always hungry. "Okay. Race you back."

They pushed each other playfully out of the way, jostling to be the first out of the hideout. Dactyl squeezed between them, and won the struggle. Once outside, Daniel carefully covered the opening and adjusted his string with the bones and tins on it. "This is my intruder alarm," he explained. Then they headed for home.

At the barn, Daniel's Dad offered Jed a ride home.

"It'll save your dad coming over." Dad held a tool in his hand. "Besides I need to return this pipe cutter to him anyway."

Jed nodded, and Dad went to start the truck.

Mom, stirring a steaming pot of his favourite home-made chicken noodle soup, greeted Daniel in the kitchen. He washed his hands quickly at the kitchen sink, and grabbed a couple of ham and cheese sandwiches from the plateful on the counter. He chomped into one and slid into his usual seat at the table beside Cheryl. He rubbed his fingers gently over her face, making her laugh and grab at his hands. Mom placed a bowl of soup in front of him.

"Slow down," she tapped him gently on the top of his head. "There's plenty of food."

He smiled at her and kept chewing. "I'm starving," he said, remembering that he'd hardly eaten any breakfast.

Being with Jed had almost made him forget about the

horror of the night before and the decisions his family faced. He tried not to think of it now. Soon enough his dad would return from driving Jed home, and the tension in the house would be back. He took a small sip of the tasty soup. She'd made it with flat noodles and big chunks of chicken and carrots, just the way he liked it.

"Mom?" he said, suddenly remembering Pederson. "I was wondering about angina."

"Angina?? What about it?" she asked, surprised.

"What causes it?" Daniel wanted to be sure Pederson was going to be okay.

"Usually, it's triggered by too much physical activity that increases the heart's demand for oxygen. So if they don't get enough oxygen they suffer an attack," she answered.

"Can someone have it for years and still be all right if they have an attack?" Daniel asked.

"Sure, if they have stable angina, and as long as they take their pills or puffer and have regular checkups," she clarified. "Why?"

He thought quickly. "Ah, I'm doing a health project for school on the human heart and I just wondered."

Mom nodded.

"So," he repeated, "if they had an attack, took their medicine and rested, they'd be fine then?"

"Yes, as long as they were healthy otherwise," she confirmed, placing the plate of sandwiches on the table in front of him.

"They'd take nitroglycerine, right?" he asked.

"Yes." Mom seemed pleased that he knew the right term. "But, if they have unstable angina, which means they have increased and unpredictable attacks, then they probably need to be hospitalized when an attack hits."

Daniel nodded, digesting the information as he slurped his soup and finished his sandwich. Pederson called his condition angina and said he had just done too much work. Surely scraping and digging in the tunnel with not much fresh air had triggered his attack. But maybe he'd better check on him as soon as he could, just to be sure.

Just then Dad came in and joined them at the table.

"So how was your ride?" he asked quietly, reaching for a sandwich.

"Good," Daniel answered. "Thanks for taking Jed home."

Dad said, "I had to return the cutter to Mr. Lindstrom anyway and it seemed like a good time."

There didn't seem to be much else to say, so with Cheryl's constant babbling and his parents' strained silence, Daniel excused himself and went to his room to think things through.

Absentmindedly, he paged through his dinosaur books, but now that he'd told Jed about his ideas, there wasn't much more he could do, except try to convince Pederson to tell people. Why was the old man still being so secretive? Anyone could see that he'd made a major discovery. Daniel would have to find out more next time he was there.

In the meantime, he moved over to his desk and picked up his math text. He had a pile of homework to do. At least it would take his mind off losing the farm. As he worked, he heard Mom put Cheryl down for her nap and go to her own room to sleep, so she'd be rested for work later. Sometimes she looked so tired these days.

Between doing homework and staring out the window, he managed to pass most of the afternoon. He'd finished his math and had just started on his essay about the rain forests in South America, when he heard Cheryl gurgling to herself. He tiptoed into her soft yellow bedroom and over to her crib.

A mobile of dancing clowns hung over her, and she was kicking at the bottom crib pad to make them move. She looked so cute, and determined. As he lifted her out, she snuggled into his neck and chewed on his hair. He whispered to her and picked up her favourite toy, his old blue teddy bear, and took her downstairs. They sat in the big armchair in the living room. When she squirmed too much, he sat her on the blanket on the floor and passed her some colourful rings and other noisy toys to play with. He liked watching her.

It wasn't too long before his Mom appeared. Daniel swept Cheryl up and handed her into Mom's outstretched arms. Cheryl obviously needed her diaper changed, but he'd leave that to the expert.

"I'm going out to do chores," he said, before Mom could even suggest it.

She smiled and patted him on the shoulder. "Thanks, Daniel!"

He joined Dad, who was already in the barn milking Lily. They did their chores in silence, except for the clanging and scraping of buckets and rustling of the cattle in their stalls as he fed and watered them. Dad's face was strained, with deep furrowed lines across his forehead. Daniel didn't want to provoke him in any way.

Later at the supper table, and afterwards when the family watched *Honey, I Shrunk the Kids* together on television, it seemed to Daniel that everyone was avoiding any mention of their problems. Only after he'd gone to bed did he hear the voices of his parents deep in discussion.

There was no way he was going to listen to their conversation tonight. He'd only hear more bad news. His thoughts wouldn't stop churning around in his head as it was. What would it be like if they had to move away? When would they have to go? They just couldn't! How could he convince Pederson to speak up before it was too late? But even if he did announce his discoveries, would it be soon enough to do anything about their farm? Would his parents or the bank manager understand the possibilities for their own place?

He slept fitfully all night, working himself into a fevered state. He woke up sweating at four a.m. and threw the quilt off. Exhaustion took over again and he

eventually fell back asleep, but only when he turned his thoughts to when he was little and doing fun things with his grandparents. On the farm, of course.

CHAPTER EIGHT

On Monday morning, winter daylight came, frosty and bright, as Daniel hurried up the lane to wait for the school bus on the access road. A brisk wind made his cheeks sting. He juggled his armload of books with his skates and eased the lunch box from banging against his left leg. He already knew this was not going to be a good day.

He was trying to imagine not living on the farm anymore, and failing miserably. He shook his head. He couldn't envision not being able to roam in the nearby hills, couldn't imagine not being able to visit his secret hideout. This place was so much a part of him and who he was, how could he ever leave it behind? How could he leave Gypsy? And just before Christmas, too. With impatience, he brushed a wave of hair out of his eyes. If only none of this were happening.

Everything was changing, everything that meant so much to him. Would Dad really sell the land? That would destroy everything Daniel had been dreaming about. He took a deep breath to calm himself. Maybe he was worrying for nothing. Maybe they really wouldn't do it. Dad had said it was just a possibility, if things didn't improve financially.

But Daniel knew his dad had been having meetings at the bank for the last several months. Each time he returned home, he looked glummer and glummer. But Daniel had figured that it wasn't critical and somehow they would make everything come out all right. They always had before. A queasy feeling told him that this time was different. His parents were definitely serious about selling the farm.

He took another deep breath to quell his stomach's lurching. Slowly exhaling, he surveyed the yard as he waited for the bus. His eyes caught the trees along the edge of the gravel road on the opposite side of the house. Or what remained of the trees. He'd almost forgotten about the wreckage, even though he'd been mighty upset when he'd come home from school and found the mess. It had happened late in the fall.

A ruthless road maintenance crew had removed them, they said, to make way for a wider improved road and a deeper drainage ditch. After that, the weather had turned cold and stormy and they'd just left the twisted piles of earth and torn branches until next spring. He had no idea why his father hadn't gone ahead and moved them. Maybe it had something to do with the trees having been planted as seedlings in two neat rows by his caring great-grandfather many years ago.

He shuddered now as he looked at the gaping holes left by the uprooted spruce and caragana. To him, the scarred landscape looked as if someone had slashed a knife across a painted masterpiece. It was just as bad. He felt like someone had stabbed him, too. He sighed and climbed on board the big yellow bus that had just screeched to a halt in front of him.

All day he fidgeted in school, trying to think of a way his family could keep living on the farm. And how could he convince Pederson to announce his finds? Lost in thought, he barely realized when his class began rehearsing the play for the Christmas concert until everyone fell silent waiting for him to say his lines. He was playing the part of Scrooge in *The Christmas Carol*. Once he remembered the lines and delivered them, he got right into it. At the end he was surprised by everyone clapping at how well he'd portrayed being miserable. If only they knew.

He tried harder to pay attention, but by the end of the afternoon in Math class he'd have had detention, except that the supervising teacher had to coach a basketball game. He let Daniel off with a stern warning. Daniel breathed a sigh of relief and escaped. At least for the time being. When he got home the fatal decision might be made.

He was barely aware he was riding the school bus for

home until it slowed approaching his stop. That's when he spotted the For Sale signs leaning against the workshop in the yard.

He jumped down from the bus and ran. He burst through the barn door, nearly stepping on a kitten. He ran down the length of the barn until he found Dad in a stall with Lily. Dad sat on the milking stool with the half-filled pail at his feet, staring into space.

"No, we can't go," Daniel choked out. He stood against the railing, struggling to swallow the hard lump rising in his throat. "There must be something more we can do."

"Danny, I know you're devastated, Son, but there's no alternative," said Dad, recovering from the shock of Daniel's abrupt entrance. He continued quietly, without energy, "We've already explained this. You're just going to have to get used to the idea. Like the rest of us."

"I don't want us to go," Daniel repeated stubbornly. Then more defiantly, he declared, "I won't go."

Nothing could justify leaving the only home they'd ever known. Their animals. He would never sell Gypsy or leave Dactyl behind. And what about Jed? And his secret hiding place? What was wrong with Dad? He had never been a quitter. So why give up now?

"Please be reasonable." Dad sounded exhausted. "There isn't much hope in farming anymore, Son. It's the same all over the prairies. We just have to face facts." He rose and carried the pail to the milking room. He'd forgotten to take the stool. Daniel followed behind with it.

"Face facts? You haven't even given anything else a chance," he criticized, shoving the stool against a wall near the milking-room door. "I know times haven't been so good, but there has to be something we can do. What about you taking a job off the farm for a while? Maybe on the oil rigs or something."

"I looked into that, Daniel, but I'm too old to get on the rigs. And work on the highway crews doesn't start until the late spring. I don't have much education, and there's no work around here. We'll have to move someplace where I'll have a shot at finding something. And where your mom can get a better-paying nursing job, too." Dad shook his head and concluded in a quiet voice, "The only way is to sell. Sounds like the Nelwins are interested in buying our place."

"No, you can't be serious," Daniel blindly stumbled to the feed room, fighting back tears. The decision seemed final. *I won't cry, I won't,* he told himself as Dactyl ran to him with his tail wagging excitedly. Jumping on his chest, the dog licked his face. Daniel's arms tightened around his pet for several minutes.

"Come on boy," he said eventually, his voice cracked and muffled. "Let's go feed Gypsy."

Mechanically, he fed his horse and patted her muzzle. As Daniel talked to Gypsy in a soothing voice, Dactyl sniffed about the barn. Then Daniel noticed that his dad had left the door open to the milk separating room, with the pails of fresh milk sitting on the floor. The kittens were already heading in that direction. He hurried over to close the door, then turned to watch Dad leave. His shoulders were slumped and he seemed to shuffle instead of stepping quickly. It was like he had nowhere to go. There was something definitely wrong with him.

Daniel fed the rest of the cattle, and then moved mounds of straw around the stall with the pitchfork and readjusted Gypsy's pail of water several times. Finally though, he had no other reason to stay. He closed the stable door as quietly as he could. Outside, glancing at the house, he decided he wasn't ready for another confrontation, especially with Mom, who he could see in the kitchen window preparing supper.

Instead, he headed on foot for the wood-covered hills behind the barn. He'd visit his hideout for a few minutes before dark and try to come up with a plan. He peered at the dark smudges of cloud streaked across the indigo sky.

He picked up a stick and threw it. Dactyl sprang to retrieve it. Again and again, Daniel threw the stick as they crossed the pasture. He was oblivious to his changing surroundings and the leaden sky. After awhile, the golden retriever grew tired of fetching the branch. He was more intent on sniffing out animal tracks instead.

Then suddenly, Dactyl caught a fresh scent and bounded off through the bush in frenzied pursuit. Lost in thought, Daniel hardly noticed the dog disappear, nor did he see the buildup of threatening clouds to the west, until the first snow crystals stung his face.

"Dactyl, come on, boy. It's time to get back," he shouted. The increasing wind flipped the ties from his parka hood into his face. "Here, boy."

He repeatedly called Dactyl to come. He could hear the yips of the dog closing in on his prey. There was no calling him back now; Daniel would just have to wait until he tired and returned to him. That's when he noticed that the heavily falling snow was making everything look a deceptive white.

Urgently, he began calling his dog again, but the escalating pitch of the wind blew his voice away before it could reach Dactyl's ears. He would just have to start back without him. Dactyl would find his own way. As he turned for home, the snow began coming down more thickly, and the wind increased. He squinted and bowed his head to keep the driving snow out of his face, plodding forward.

All at once, he realized he wasn't sure anymore which way to go. The trail of footprints he'd made through the snow had disappeared and he couldn't see a foot in front of him! The intensifying snowfall and blustering wind obscured his vision. It was getting dark. He peered into the blankness. Should he head instead to his hideout? When he turned around there was only a white wall.

He gasped as an icy blast of wind took his breath away. Eddies of snow swirled all around him. Jerking his toque down over his numb forehead, he nestled his chin as far down as it would go into his coat collar. Turning, he thought he'd retrace his trail, but as quickly as he had stepped, his footsteps had disappeared in the blowing snow.

He trudged on, stumbling through the shifting snow, hoping he was headed towards home. Hunger pangs gnawed at his middle, but all he found in his pockets were a couple of sticks of gum. He couldn't take his mitts off to open them. If he could find his cave, he should be snug until the storm blew over. He'd be able to eat those chocolate bars and beef jerky he had stashed in the old coffee tin for an emergency, too. At the time, he hadn't imagined anything as serious as the blizzard howling around him now.

Blindly he pushed on, staggering through the knee-deep drifts, wallowing and falling and rising again. Where was Dactyl? He hoped he was all right in a natural shelter somewhere. Or maybe he'd gone home and someone was right this minute out looking for Daniel. On the other hand, where would they look? Daniel couldn't see a thing with the snow stinging his eyes. How could anyone see him?

Almost at that instant, he tripped over a branch. He fell on his knees against a tree, gasping. The snow continually swirled around him, and a gust of wind blew some inside his coat collar and down the back of his neck, making him shiver even more. Then he thought he glimpsed a shaft of light through the trees. Great! He would head that way. Maybe it was the yardlight and he wasn't far from home.

Dragging himself to his feet, he continued to struggle along, clapping his hands together to keep the numbness away. The more he walked though, the farther away the light seemed to be, until abruptly it disappeared and he knew he was lost. Urgently, he began calling Dactyl, again and again. But there was no answering bark.

His thoughts jumbled and crashed together. He knew he must stay calm. *Think,* he reminded himself. What had he learned last year in 4-H about wilderness survival? Hadn't even pioneers known enough to dig themselves into a snowbank to keep warm?

As icy crystals stung him, he spotted a likely looking snowed-under embankment. He fell to his knees and frantically began burrowing into the drift. From out of nowhere, Dactyl whimpered and scrabbled in the deep whiteness beside him. The dog seemed to sense the urgency and pawed into the snowbank next to him.

Clawing and scooping handful after handful of the drifted snow, Daniel was making progress, but he was also beginning to tire. *Mustn't stop, mustn't fall asleep. Whistle!* He tried, but could only hiss through his teeth. Then, puffing and grunting, he struggled to carve out a circular shelter.

How deep should he tunnel? His dog whined. Daniel had to make the indentation big enough for both him and Dactyl to crawl into.

Ouch! His mittened hand hit something hard. A rock? No, it sounded hollow. More like some sort of wood, maybe boards with an empty space behind them. He clawed faster, uncovering a knob. It was an old door of some sort! What was a door doing out here?

With a shock, Daniel realized he had no idea where he was. He only knew he'd come a long way and he really needed to find a good shelter, and fast. As it was, he could hardly feel his legs, feet, and hands. He was exhausted and chilled to the bone. He could freeze to death if he didn't get warm soon. And he didn't want to be alone in this maelstrom. He cleared away more snow, then began pounding on the wooden slab with his mittened fists.

"Help! Somebody help me!" he yelled, hammering on the boards. As he tried kicking at the door, tingling slivers of cold shot into his numbed feet. Why wouldn't anyone answer? Of course! The door had been buried in snow. It was probably never used. Maybe it was just an old root cellar. Or maybe it didn't lead anywhere. What if it wasn't even a door? Just a piece of scrap? What was he going to do?

Abruptly a heavy padded hand or paw grasped his shoulder and spun him around. Daniel gaped at the snow-encrusted mass. His whole body shuddered. Who or what was it? Then he heard a low growl. He cowered. Why wasn't Dactyl reacting? What was he going to do?

CHAPTER NINE

All at once, exhaustion overcame Daniel. He sagged. Even Dactyl seemed too tired to fight. They all stood frozen. Then Daniel took a peek. He still couldn't make sense of the looming shape. Then he heard another growl. All at once, the one figure separated into two. Bear and Pederson!

Bear whined, watching Pederson.

"Oh, it's you is it?" Pederson rasped out through a fit of coughing. "I wondered who was making all the racket at my back door. What in tarnation are you doing here on a devilish night like this?"

He didn't seem to be looking for an answer, so Daniel just stared up at him.

"We can't get in this way. Follow me, you darn-blamed young fool," Pederson gasped, once he had caught his breath. "And bring your mutt with you."

Daniel obeyed trancelike, summoning Dactyl to his side. He struggled to keep up with Pederson's disappearing back in the dark, tried to follow his footprints through the swirling layers of snow. They seemed to be circling around a huge bluff of trees that would probably lead them to the front of the old man's shack.

The further they walked, the harder Daniel gasped for breath in the freezing air. Stabs of pain jabbed at his chest. He could hear the old man's hacking coughs up ahead.

How much further? Better get to the cabin soon. His legs felt like wood. Blasts of snow blinded him.

Suddenly, he stumbled against Pederson, who had stopped and swung open a door. A second later, warmth and brightness as Daniel fell headlong into the room and sank to the floor. The smell of stew wafted over him. Dactyl crept in and crouched beside him, whining and licking his face. Daniel just wanted to lie there soaking up the heat, but Pederson bellowed at him.

"Were you born in a barn, lad? There's enough winter outside without having to bring any in here! Get up and close the door!" The old man coughed and sputtered as he reeled over to a unlit corner of the room and collapsed on an old wooden chair.

Daniel rushed to obey, even though there didn't seem to be any feeling in his feet or hands. Using his whole body, he strained to push the door shut.

Pederson, perched on the edge of the chair, was struck with another explosive fit of coughing. He held a ragged handkerchief to his mouth trying to gain control. The phlegmy choking sounds scared Daniel. What if the old man died? He scanned the room for the bottle of pills, and saw them on top of a makeshift bookshelf.

"Coffee," Pederson croaked, pointing to a tall coffee pot sitting on top of the wood stove beside a simmering pot of stew.

Daniel rushed to grab a cup off a shelf nearby and carefully poured the steaming coffee. Halfway back across the room, he stumbled and sloshed out most of it. Bear snarled menacingly as he approached Pederson with what remained. A quick tap on the head from his master silenced the dog.

The coffee delivered, Daniel backed away across the room, leaned against the door and laid a reassuring hand on Dactyl's back, not sure if Bear would keep his distance. Pederson's dog occasionally growled low in the back of his throat. He seemed to have forgotten Daniel's earlier visits, or maybe Dactyl's presence upset him. Pederson sipped at the soothing drink, then closed his eyes and leaned against the wall.

The aroma of the stew wafted Daniel's way and made his stomach rumble. An old china bowl with a matching mug sat ready and waiting next to a closed hard-covered book on a small table at Pederson's elbow. Daniel wondered if the old guy would offer him anything; he was still sagged against the wall with his eyes shut. The snow caking his outer garments was beginning to melt and water trickled onto the floor.

He still hadn't invited Daniel in any farther than the door, either, but there didn't seem to be anything else Daniel could do, except stay. He sure didn't want to go back into the storm. Besides, he'd been welcomed before. And taken into Pederson's confidence. Uncertain, he stared at the old man, who sat with his eyes closed, struggling for breath.

Suddenly, the pungent smell of dampness and mould tickled Daniel's nostrils. He sneezed. Startled, Pederson looked up.

"What are you still standing at the door for, young man? Take those wet clothes off and get near the fire," he wheezed.

Finally! Daniel relaxed. Then he inched closer to the stove and removed his toque and mitts, and slowly unzipped his parka. As he held his hands over the searing heat, Pederson grunted and removed his own outer clothing. He was breathing heavily.

Bear and Dactyl eyed each other across the floor and growled. Dactyl began to slink over to Daniel on his belly. The steam rose off his damp fur as he settled himself at the boy's feet and closed his eyes.

"Are you hungry, young man?" Pederson asked, rising slowly and shuffling over. He lifted the lid off the pot to reveal the bubbling stew.

"Yes, sir," Daniel croaked out.

Pederson dished out two servings and indicated a place at the table for Daniel. He shoved over a chair that was missing a few rungs. Silently, they ate hot chunks of venison mixed with vegetables. The meat was tender and well-seasoned. They soaked up the gravy with slabs of thick bread.

Daniel gazed around as they ate. Most of the room was in sharp shadows, being lit only by bare light bulbs. He got a better look now at the shelves nailed along most of the walls, filled with archaeology tools, books, and jars. He had a clear view, too, of the long plank table that held the dinosaur bones. He smiled to himself when he thought about Brett and Wade's stories about Pederson cutting up people. If they only knew!

When they were done eating, Pederson fed both dogs the leftovers, then sat on his chair and reached to a low cupboard beside him for his pipe and tobacco. While he was searching for matches, he had another coughing fit and set aside the smoking gear with disgust.

"What's your name?"

"Daniel, Daniel Bringham," he replied, shifting on the hard crate.

"Yes, but do you have any middle names?"

"Well, yes. My whole name is Daniel Ezekiel Alexander Bringham," Daniel answered.

"That's quite a mouthful, young fella." Pederson said, gathering the dishes from the table and placing them into a tin basin.

"I was named for both my grandfathers," Daniel added, feeling his face turn red.

"Well, now then, ah Daniel, tell me what you were doing out in that blizzard?"

"I was trying to think of a way to save our farm, and going to my secret hideout. You know the place where I met you a couple of days ago – and I couldn't find Dactyl and the storm came up and all of a sudden I was lost and, and..." The words came out in a rush.

"Whoa, whoa. Slow down some," Pederson said, as he started to cough again. "What's this about you trying to save your farm?"

"Well, remember the other day when I mentioned the oil company that wanted to lease the land?"

"Mmm-hmm."

"Well, it's gotten worse. My dad went to the bank and they said that wouldn't help any. They'll probably have to *sell*. And we'll have to move!" Daniel explained the whole problem as best he could, being careful to leave out the bit about Dad coming to ask Pederson if he could rent his pasture land. He didn't want to make him angry. He might send Daniel back into the storm.

When he finished, he thought the old man had fallen asleep, as he sat with his head down and his eyes closed.

"Sir?" Daniel asked, making a grating noise with his foot on the floor to get his attention.

"Humph," Pederson grunted. "I heard you. That's quite a problem you have, better sleep on it. There's a sleeping bag in that cupboard. You can put the two chairs we're sitting on together for a bed."

"Sir?"

"What?"

"My parents must be out looking for me! Shouldn't we phone them or something?" By now Mom and Dad would be in a panic.

"Got no phone. No one will be out in this blizzard anyway. I'll see you get home in the morning. Now, it's time to get some sleep."

Daniel stared at him. Surely there must be some way to get word to his family. But he couldn't think of anything. Not without a phone. He listened to the howling of the wind outside and knew he'd never make it if he tried to head for home now.

"Ah, Sir?"

"What now?" Pederson headed to the wood box and grabbed an armload.

"I have to go to the bathroom."

"Over there," Pederson nodded, indicating a jerry can in the corner by the door to the passageway. "That'll have to do for tonight." He stoked up the fire, loading it with wood, then climbed onto his cot.

When Daniel was finally ready for sleep, he positioned the chairs together for his bed. He found an old sleeping bag in the bottom of the cupboard and balled up his parka for a pillow just as the light was extinguished.

"Darn power's out," Pederson complained from across the darkened room.

Daniel shuddered, and swallowed hard. A power failure. He'd thought Pederson had turned off the light. The thought of being in near-total darkness with the strange old man and his unpredictable dog made him shiver. Then as his eyes adjusted, he saw there was a tiny glow from the cracks in the wood stove. Dactyl curled on the floor beside him. Daniel reached out an arm and curled his fingers into his fur. That was better. But he sure hoped his parents weren't out looking for him. Anything could happen in that blizzard.

His primitive bed was hard and uncomfortable, but although he tried to stay awake in case someone was out looking for him, he was too exhausted. The warmth from the fire, and the roar of the wind circling the little cabin soon lulled him to sleep.

CHAPTER TEN

A wild nattering and screeching woke Daniel several hours later. He lay gasping in the murky darkness, trying to figure out where he was and whether he was having a nightmare or was actually awake. In moments, he realized he was in Pederson's cabin. The horrible sounds were coming from the old man. He was thrashing around on his cot as he coughed and muttered in his sleep.

Daniel tiptoed over and shook him, but he kept tossing and shaking. Bear whimpered at the foot of the bed. "Mr. Pederson, Mr. Pederson, wake up. You're having a bad dream."

By the glow of the fire coming from the vent in the stove, Daniel could see Pederson's face. Streams of sweat ran down his flushed forehead, mingling with tears. His pillow was damp. He was in some kind of feverish shaking fit! What should Daniel do? It was his fault entirely. Pederson must have gotten worse, being out in the storm to rescue him. What if he died? Daniel had to do something.

Dactyl stirred and padded over, nuzzling his head under Daniel's hand for a pet. Daniel absentmindedly scratched his head while his thoughts whirred.

Tea, that was it. Camomile tea, or mint tea, or what? He remembered stories Mom had told him of his great-grandparents in the pioneering days, how they brewed up teas made from local plants. Surely he could find something in all those containers on the shelves.

Dactyl whined.

"Go lie down boy," Daniel pointed to his spot by the makeshift bed. "I have work to do." Dactyl gave Daniel a concerned look, then obeyed. He skirted Bear and settled back down on the floor.

Daniel opened up the vent on the stove so that a shaft of light angled across the floor and to the top of the shelves. He scanned the row of jars. He'd try camomile tea. His grandmother had pointed out the wild plants growing all over the farmyard so he knew they were a yellowish colour. Ah, that looked like it. But wait – what if this wasn't really camomile and he killed the old man by mistake?

He suddenly remembered the other day when Brett and Craig had teased him on the bus. He had been scared Pederson planned to poison him, and now he might be poisoning the old guy instead! Pederson might be gruff around the edges, but the poor man wouldn't poison anyone! All that these jars contained were herbs and the makings for tea. Even so, Daniel knew from something Mom had said that they could be dangerous if he used too much or the wrong thing. Should he give it a try anyway?

Convulsive coughs and more wailings from the bed convinced him. At the rate things were going, it didn't matter if he gave Pederson the wrong tea or not. By the sounds coming from him, he wasn't doing too well.

Daniel fumbled around in the cupboard for a pan and filled it from the pail by the door. Then he set it on the stove and threw some more sticks on the fire. As he waited for the water to boil, he found himself quaking a little at his predicament. Here he was in a strange place in the middle of a blizzard with a sick and ranting man. But things could be worse, he realized with a start. At least he was in out of the storm, and he might actually be able to help Pederson. Dactyl slunk back over and lay at his feet.

Splashes of water sizzling on the surface of the stove alerted Daniel that the water was ready. He opened the jar and sniffed. How many of these dried flowers should he use? Might as well make it good and strong. He dumped half the jarful into the boiling water, then went in search of a cup.

By the time the tea was steeped, he had found some candles and matches and lit them. Pederson's rantings had become louder. Bear seemed uneasy at Daniel's approach to his master, but at a sharp "lie still," he settled back down with a whimper. Dactyl padded to his sleeping spot.

Daniel struggled to raise Pederson's head and pour tea into his mouth. At first most of the warm liquid dribbled down his chin, but eventually he managed to get him to swallow some. It helped the coughing subside and as he mopped the old man's brow with a damp cloth, Pederson seemed to calm down. Every once in a while, he mumbled about "his sweet Marianna," and coughed intermittently.

Crawling back onto his chair-bed, Daniel lay looking at the wavering patterns of light on the ceiling. Suddenly, he bounded back up again. He'd forgotten to turn down the stove vent and blow out the candles. Back in his sleeping bag, he listened to Pederson's feverish mumbling and worried about his parents. He'd been pretty hard on Dad in the barn just before he took off. He should have gone in for supper. If only he could let them know he was all right. He reached down and patted Dactyl's head. His dog gave an answering whimper.

The flickerings on the ceiling made him think of blinking lights on Christmas trees. Christmas was only a month away. He didn't want it to be the last one they ever spent on the farm. He'd have to come up with a plan. Something definite. As he drifted off into a fitful sleep, he hoped his parents were home safe with Cheryl, not out looking for him.

He awoke stiff and sore in the morning. At least he thought it was morning. It was hard to tell what time it was in the shadowy gloom of the shack, and he'd been up and down all night. He peeked over at Pederson. His breathing was laboured and raspy, but he lay still. Good, he was sleeping. Daniel felt a flush of satisfaction over his successful doctoring. He'd been up several times giving the old guy tea.

Suddenly, his grin disappeared. Oh no, what if Pederson were unconscious instead? He sprang up and raced over to check. The old man's face was almost as white as the enamel dipper hanging on the wall. His fever was gone. In fact, he felt almost cool to the touch. And his gurgling breaths scared Daniel. He had to do something. He could still hear the wind howling outside, so going anywhere was out of the question. If only he could remember what his grandmother did when his grandfather had bad chest colds. Of course, a mustard plaster.

He searched the shelves, then rummaged through the cupboard until he found dry mustard and a small bag of flour. He had no idea what proportions to use, but he mixed the dry ingredients with water until they felt pasty, like papier mâché, and spread it over a handkerchief that he found in a drawer. Then he set it on Pederson's bare chest and kept checking to make sure the skin wasn't getting too red, just like he remembered his grandmother doing. Once he removed the hankie a few minutes later, he found another quilt in the cupboard and tucked it tight up around Pederson's neck.

Both dogs were whining at the door by then, so he

pried it open to let them out. As he did, a huge mound of snow that had been packed against the door fell into the room. The blizzard was still gusting, throwing ice crystals into his face. There was no way in the world he could go home in that. Even the dogs hesitated before creeping out. He swept out the snow and slammed the door shut after them, before going to look for some breakfast for himself.

He was just spreading some Saskatoon berry jam that he'd found onto a thick slice of bread, when the whining and scratchings of the dogs drew him back to the door. They were covered in snow, their coats matted with ice. Both settled down beside the stove to dry off. Pederson continued to sleep.

Once Daniel finished eating he began to inspect the contents of the cabin a little more closely. His attention was caught by the set of texts on the top of the bookshelf. They were scientific books on geology, paleontology, and archaeology. He drew one down. It was more technical and harder to read than his own books. He pulled a few more down, and then he noticed a stack of magazines. He grabbed several and sat down at the table to look through them. Most had no pictures, just articles. As hard to read as the text books. On one back cover, he noticed the address label: Dr. O. I. B. Pederson.

The old man was a doctor of some kind – probably paleontology. That's what Daniel wanted to be – an expert! But why would a little disagreement at one museum make him want to live here like a hermit?

Weren't there other museums? Or was he really just retired? The thought puzzled him as he flipped through more of the magazines, but he found no answers. While searching the shelves, he did find a dog-eared herbal remedy book that Mr. Pederson obviously used in conjunction with his collection of dried flowers and plants.

Throughout the morning, the blizzard still raged outside. Whenever Daniel opened the door to peer into the hazy bleakness he was met with buffeting winds and blowing snow. The windows had long since been covered in hoarfrost and the drifts reached more than halfway up the side of the cabin walls. Daniel, Pederson, and the dogs were snug enough inside. The wood box was full, and although the power was still out there were plenty of candles, a couple of flashlights, and a kerosene lamp.

What concerned Daniel most was the thought of his parents worrying about him, but there was nothing he could do to let them know he was safe. It would be foolish to venture out. He sure didn't want to be lost in the storm again. He'd just have to wait it out!

Every once in a while, he wondered what Jed was doing. Had Daniel's parents called Jed's family to join in the search? Jed would sure think he was dumb to get caught in a blizzard.

Later, he wrestled with Dactyl and Bear. The two dogs play-growled at one another from time to time, but otherwise seemed to be getting along fine.

When he got tired of looking through the books and

magazines, Daniel ventured over to the table full of bones. Some of them were labelled. Taking a peek to see that Pederson's eyes were closed, he gently picked a relic up and examined it. As he set it down carefully again, he noticed a large fragment of rock with the rippled fossilized remains of an eggshell. He quivered with excitement at what he held in his hand, and at what lay in the ground only a few yards away. Now all he had to do was make sure Pederson got better, then convince him to speak up. He didn't know which was the bigger challenge.

He tended Pederson throughout the day, laying damp cloths on his brow, brewing various teas and helping him to the jerry can whenever necessary. As time progressed, his colour looked more normal and he seemed to rest easier, although he still had the hacking cough. By mid-afternoon he felt well enough to sit up when Daniel brought him some scrambled eggs and bread to eat.

"Where did you learn to cook?"

"I've known how to cook for ages – ever since I was young. My mom believes it's important for a guy to learn, too. It's not just up to the women these days you know."

"That's good advice, young fella, and these are mighty good eggs," said Pederson in a hoarse whisper. Once he had finished eating, he handed Daniel the almost empty plate. "That's all I can manage."

Daniel fed the leftovers to the dogs, and returned the plate to the table. Pederson settled back onto his pillow and drew the blankets up around his chin. "Tell me again about your problem with your farm. And don't leave anything out."

So Daniel explained the circumstances as best as he could, including his dad's meetings with the bank, and Pederson listened with closed eyes, nodding once in awhile.

"I really want to stay here," Daniel concluded. "And that's why I came over the other day. I really need to be able to prove that there are dinosaurs here to convince my dad that he has to keep this land."

"Ah, I understand, lad. And I'm sorry, I can't help you. Now is just not the right time to announce the discovery."

"I see." Daniel sat with his head hung for a few moments, disappointed with Pederson's response, trying to respect his need for privacy. But it didn't seem fair. He got up and walked over to the stove, where he stoked the fire and threw in another log.

A few moments elapsed. "Ah, sir?" he asked hesitantly.

"Yes."

"I know you want to keep your discovery quiet for awhile, but I just don't understand exactly why."

"Well for starters, I'd like to finish the dig myself. I don't want any outside interference," said Pederson, coughing into his handkerchief. "There'd be swarms of people hovering around."

"Maybe we could stop that happening by just not letting anyone on your land," Daniel suggested.

"No, there's always somebody who wants special access or sneaks in," Pederson rasped.

Daniel nodded in defeat. Suddenly he noticed the stack of magazines on the table. "Sir," he asked, feeling a little guilty that he hadn't put them away. "I, ah, was looking in those magazines, and I saw your name on the label. What does O. I. B. stand for?"

"My parents named me Olaf Ingmar Borje Pederson," he answered with a grimace, "After both *my* grandfathers."

"That's quite a mouthful," said Daniel, and they both laughed.

"So, you're a doctor?"

"Yes, of paleontology," Pederson admitted. He blew his nose before continuing. "I've worked for various museums, but I was fed up with all the red tape and the runaround. I wanted to spend time on this area of research and the directors wanted to spend the museum's money on other things. We just didn't see eye to eye," he explained. Then he went into a coughing fit, and Daniel rushed to get him some water.

After he'd had a drink, Daniel helped him back to his bed, where he dozed off again with a disturbing rattle in his chest with each breath he took. Daniel hovered over him anxiously for a while, and then resumed his study of the bones and fossils.

By late afternoon the ferocity of the storm seemed to have let up and Daniel peered out. There was still light snow eddying around, but he decided it should be safe for him to go home. The only thing was, he couldn't leave Pederson behind. He was still too sick. He went to wake him.

"You have to come with me," Daniel insisted. "I can't leave you here."

But looking the frail man over, Daniel wondered how they could make it.

"I can't walk that far, lad," Pederson said weakly from the bed. "I'd just be a burden to you."

"We'll figure out something. Let me look around." Daniel debated about the best way as he donned his outside gear. If only he had Gypsy. Or the snowmobile.

The dogs got excited and started barking and bouncing around when they realized Daniel was heading out. They almost knocked him over in the commotion. Trying to restrain them, the answer struck him.

"Do you have a toboggan of some sort?" he quizzed Pederson.

The old man thought for a moment. "Yes, I do," he replied. "An old one. It should be leaning against the side of the cabin." He gasped for breath. "But you'll have to dig for it."

"Not a problem," said Daniel, going to the door.

"Wait, young man. You can't possibly pull me that whole distance," Pederson croaked out.

Daniel grinned. "I don't have to." He pointed to the dogs.

Pederson smiled back, as he tried to catch his breath.

"I've used Bear for that kind of thing in the past, but I don't know how the two of them will be together."

"We'll find out!"

Daniel stepped outside and staggered through the deep bank to the side of the cabin. He found a stick and began knocking the snow away from a pile of old boards. With a little effort and a few hard tugs, he managed to drag the toboggan from the bottom of the pile and over to the door. Then he searched for ropes or anything else he figured would work as a harness for the dogs.

When he went back inside, Pederson was sitting up pulling on a second pair of socks. The effort made him breathe heavily. Daniel grabbed the blankets, the sleeping bag, and a pillow. Then taking an old cloth off the fossil table, he wrapped a flashlight, a candle, and some matches, and hauled everything outside. He spread one blanket out on the toboggan, then the sleeping bag and the pillow. He placed the other wrapped package at the bottom of the sleeping bag.

Then he went back for Pederson, pulling him up gently from the bed and helping him bundle into his parka and mitts. He made sure he had his heart pills. Then together they staggered outside, but the exertion caused Pederson to go into a bout of coughing.

Daniel helped him onto the toboggan, then zipped him into the sleeping bag. He realized he also needed to secure him, because he was seriously weakened and not able to hold on. He ran back into the cabin and found another rope. He tied it around the old man's middle to hold him in place, then laid the second blanket over him.

"Wait, just a minute," Pederson sputtered. "A compass. We'll need that. There's one on the corner of the table with the fossils."

Daniel nodded and ran back into the shack to get it. He stuffed it into his jacket pocket, turned down the stove, and closed the door securely behind him. By now, it had started to snow again and the wind had picked up. They'd have to hurry.

Quickly, Daniel hooked up Dactyl, and then, after a bit of persuasion, Bear. He led them forward, dropping back to check on Pederson as they jolted ahead. The two dogs seemed eager to get on with their venture, and although they collided a few times at the beginning, they managed to drag the weight of their cargo. Pederson lay quietly with his hat pulled down around his eyes, as they bumped along the rough snow-covered terrain.

As they travelled, the sky darkened, and the wind blew stronger. Daniel encouraged the dogs to keep moving.

"We'll have to hurry, the storm is getting strong again," Daniel yelled back to Pederson, who nodded wearily without opening his eyes.

Daniel continued to lead the dogs over the hills towards his farm, but darkness was falling and the snow was really coming down now. He stopped at what he thought was the crest of a hill, and pulled out the compass. He tapped it.

"What's wrong?" Pederson coughed and sputtered.

"I can't see where I'm going," Daniel replied. "I don't know where I am for sure. There's something wrong with the compass." He tapped it again.

Pederson tried to talk, but the wind took his breath away and brought on another coughing fit. Daniel bundled the blanket to cover Pederson's face as best he could, and started forward again. He felt the edge of panic creeping into the pit of his stomach. It was almost totally dark. Suddenly, as the wind gusted and snow swirled about them, he knew they were lost.

"Now what'll we do?" He looked back at Pederson, but the old man seemed unaware of what was happening.

"Oh, man. Why'd you have to go limp on me?" Daniel moaned to himself. He had to make a decision. "I've got to get you off here. We need shelter."

He unhooked the dogs, and began digging into the side of a hill. He had just started to attack the snowdrift when all of a sudden he heard the roar of a distant Ski-Doo. He began to jump up and down, waving his arms.

"We're here," he yelled. "We're over here. Help! We're here."

Light from the snowmobile shone dimly in the distance. Daniel yelled even more frantically and the dogs barked, but to no avail. The howling wind made it impossible for anyone to hear them. Abruptly, the Ski-Doo disappeared. In a few moments, even the sound was gone. Daniel sank to his knees. His eyes stung with tears of frustration.

But after a minute, he rose and went back to his desperate burrowing. There was no door this time, though. When he'd managed to carve out a little hollow, he untied Pederson, and gently nudged him.

"Mr. Pederson. Mr. Pederson." Daniel began shaking him, but got no response. He huddled close to the old man, with his arm around him, trying to keep them both warm. The dogs burrowed into the hole as close as they could to the two of them. A full-blown blizzard raged about them.

"Geez, we can't just stay here. I have to get help," Daniel gasped. "Can't leave you. What are we going to do?"

CHAPTER ELEVEN

Daniel began piling snow around Pederson, trying to keep him warm. Again, he thought he could hear the intermittent sound of a snowmobile in the distance. When he stood up he could momentarily see faint shapes moving. Quickly, he found the flashlight and switched it on. Then he started to yell and jump up and down, as he waved the light. He ran in the direction of the sound, which seemed to be coming closer. Then he saw a flickering glimmer through the snow.

He waved the flashlight and screamed hysterically, "Help! We're over here. Help!"

Suddenly, a snowmobile appeared, right in front of him. He had to jump out of the way. Dad! Daniel leapt into his arms as the dogs danced in frenzied circles around them.

"Thank God, I found you!" said Dad, hugging him tight. "Let's get you home."

"No wait, Dad. It's Mr. Pederson. He's sick. He's over there."

Dad followed as he struggled through the storm to where Pederson lay in the carved-out snowdrift. Together they lifted and half-carried him to the machine. With numb fingers, Daniel helped Dad secure Pederson on board, using a length of rope from the toboggan. Then Daniel climbed onto the seat behind him. Dad tugged his cellphone from his pocket and tried calling the other searchers.

He yelled into the crackling phone. "Doug? Doug, I've found him." He waited. "I've got Pederson, too. Doug?" He listened again. "Yeah. He's sick." He nodded. "Okay. Please let Libby know. Okay, see you soon."

Daniel's dad squeezed on board in front of Pederson, made sure everyone was secure, then revved the motor. Slowly, they started making their way across country, but the thick snow made it difficult to see as the wind blustered around them.

All at once, Dad stopped and turned to Daniel. He shouted over the idling engine and wind, "With this load we aren't making very good time. And visibility is almost zero." He shook his head. "We're going to have to find shelter and wait out the storm."

Daniel nodded, then he thought he made out the clinking of cans and bones between gusts. They must be near his hideout! Very near! He tapped Dad on the back.

"Right there! I know a place." Daniel pointed in the

direction of the sound. "Hear it?"

Dad nodded, and idled down the motor until they were barely crawling along. He stopped to listen. Moments later, they reached Daniel's hideout.

Daniel jumped off the snowmobile and fought against the storm to clear the opening. The dogs scampered inside as Daniel and his dad struggled to help Pederson. His dad crawled in first, wrapped his arms around the old man's chest, and pulled, while Daniel pushed from behind. At last, they all collapsed into the silent, safe darkness.

"I'll light a candle as soon as I catch my breath," said Daniel, flopping onto his back and stretching out onto the floor of the cavern. His body was cramped and cold.

Pederson lay still, except for the heaving of his chest and another coughing fit that overtook him. Daniel crawled over to his stash of candles and matches and before long he had a couple lit. Then he brushed out the little pile of snow that had fallen in the roof opening. The dogs explored the cave, while his dad went back out to the snowmobile.

Then Dad dragged in blankets and a thermos. When he opened the container, a waft of hot chocolate hit Daniel's nose and his stomach rumbled. Dad offered him some, but he shook his head and pointed instead to Pederson.

"Give it to him. I'll get some wood and we can light a fire."

While Dad made Pederson more comfortable and

gave him a cupful of the hot chocolate, Daniel crawled outside for suitable firewood. He dragged some branches into the cave, then tried breaking them into little pieces, but they were wet. He scanned his hideout, looking over his collection of antlers, coffee tins full of rocks, and other treasures, but there didn't seem to be anything that would make good kindling.

"Dad, do you have any paper or something that we could start a fire with? This wood is soaked."

Dad searched in his pockets and then checked the saddlebags on the Ski-Doo. All he found was a crumpled repair bill.

"We'll have to make this do," he said, returning to Daniel's side.

Daniel felt over the ground looking for dry twigs. He managed to find a handful. Using the candles to keep the wood heated until it dried enough to burn on its own, he and Dad finally lit a small fire. Then they sat huddled in blankets and old sleeping bags, feeding the wavering flame.

"I have water we could heat and drink, if we had something to cook it in," said Dad, now that the hot chocolate was gone.

"I have just the thing." Daniel's teeth chattered as he searched for an old pan. Wait – his stash of chocolate bars and the beef jerky! He'd forgotten all about them.

"Nice touch," Dad said, as Daniel handed out chocolate bars and then gave some jerky to the dogs.

It wasn't long before they had a nice little blaze going. Dad dug his cellphone out of his pocket, and dialed, but it was dead. He moved closer to the doorway and tried again. Daniel could hear the crackling from where he sat, but there was no connection. Finally, Dad crawled outside into the blasting wind and dialed again.

"Libby? I can't hear you at all, but I hope you can hear me. We're in a safe place, waiting out the storm," he shouted. "We'll be okay!" Then the phone died.

Dad came in on his knees. "I'm going to pull the snowmobile into the opening – at least as far as I can. To protect the motor so we can start it later." He struggled with it for a few minutes, then seemed satisfied.

For some time Daniel and Dad sat by their mini-fire in the middle of the hideout, with Pederson lying beside it under a blanket. They all sipped hot water.

"Quite a place you have here, Daniel," Dad remarked appreciatively, peering around at the bones, pails of rocks, and other paraphernalia.

Daniel grinned.

"You find all this?" Dad asked.

"Yes." Daniel reached into his pocket and handed Dad the taculite fossil. Dad cupped it in his hands.

"So what's this? The markings almost look like the head of a sunflower."

"A fossil from a receptaculites." Daniel explained its significance.

Dad raised his eyebrows, peered around the hideout

again and then stared back down at the fossil. "So is this why you didn't want the land leased to the oil drillers, or for us to sell the farm? You have a pretty special place here."

"Does this mean you'll change your mind?" Daniel asked excitedly.

"I doubt it very much, Danny. I mean, what you have here is interesting, but nothing really substantial. Nothing that would make a real impact on the outside world."

Daniel sighed. "But Dad, this could mean so much more is out here. Edmontosauruses and other duckbills.... And if we could prove that, who knows how important the land would be then? We could open up a museum, and charge people to go on digs, and all kinds of things to make money."

"That's only a pipe dream, Danny – you don't have anything but this little chunk of rock," Dad objected. "Besides there's already the T-rex Discovery Centre at Eastend and the big museum at Drumheller. They took years to develop, and plenty of money. Who knows if you'd ever find anything really significant? Looking could take years. We need to make payments right away."

Daniel looked down at the ground, discouraged.

Suddenly, Pederson grunted. His voice crackled and he tried to clear the phlegm out of his throat. "Can't do it," he sputtered and coughed.

"Pardon?" Daniel's dad leaned over him.

"Can't lease or sell," the old man gasped out.

Dad looked at Daniel to see if he'd understood Pederson's words.

Daniel shook his head.

"Don't sell or lease your land," Pederson croaked out again.

Dad turned back to him, "Why not?"

"Tell him, Daniel," he whispered.

Daniel looked at Pederson in amazement.

"Are you sure?" he asked.

Pederson nodded and closed his eyes.

"Well, Dad, you see it's this way." Daniel's voice shook. "Mr. Pederson is a real paleontologist – Doctor Pederson – and he's found an Edmontosaurus. But even better, the skeleton is wrapped around a nest, and there's a baby skeleton! Nothing like this has ever been found before anywhere!" Daniel stopped to catch his breath.

It was clear from Dad's face that this time he did realize the importance of the find.

"This means we'd be able to have tour expeditions. Or maybe have the land declared an archaeological heritage site." Excitement raced through Daniel. "There's so much we could do! The bank just *has* to cut us some slack!"

"That's telling him, lad." Pederson wheezed out and grinned, patting Daniel's hand.

Dad laughed. "I don't know what to say. You two are quite the pair."

Then he looked at the fire and turned serious. "But you seem to have forgotten a few things. It takes a great deal of money to fund these sorts of excavations. It's a major investment just to get a research station operational, never mind a real museum. Not to mention the biggest drawback: the find is on Mr. Pederson's land, not ours."

Startled, Daniel felt the bottom drop out of his stomach. He hadn't thought about that!

Pederson added breathlessly, "I'm convinced there are other sites – close by." He coughed. "Right on your land."

"Where?" Dad asked.

"Right where you thought, Daniel." Pederson coughed again. "The spot you pointed out to me the first day you came to my place."

"YES!!" Daniel shouted, startling the dogs, who began barking and wagging their tails.

"I have another one marked, too, not far from my cabin." Pederson winked at him.

Daniel stared at him in surprise. "The white cross?"

Pederson nodded.

Daniel breathed deeply and grinned. The dream had been right. The cross hadn't marked Mrs. Pederson's grave like they'd all thought!

His dad chuckled. "Well, I have to say, you two seem to have it all figured out. But I'm not totally won over yet. And I don't know that we'll be able to convince the bank to turn your schemes into money, but it's sure worth a try. We don't have anything to lose."

Daniel hugged him and grinned at Pederson. Then over the course of the next hour, he highlighted his adventures for Dad. He explained how even though Pederson had been really sick, he had ventured out in the storm to rescue Daniel. For his part, the old man was all praises for Daniel's healing abilities, and for having saved him the first time in the tunnel.

"I'm proud of you, Son," Dad said, hugging Daniel around the shoulders. "You've done well. I've been just sick about losing all that my grandfather and his father worked for."

Daniel felt warm all over. Then his father offered to have Pederson stay with them until he was entirely well again.

"You'll have your own personal caregiver," Dad informed him. "My wife's a nurse."

Pederson grimaced. "I'm sure I'll be fine, once I've been watered and fed and had a good night's sleep."

"We all will!" Dad laughed. "Still, the offer is open for you to stay as long as you need."

"Thank, you. I appreciate the invitation, but I'm sure I'll be on my way tomorrow."

Daniel smiled and snuggled into his blanket, listening to the storm raging outside and the muted voices of Dad and Mr. Pederson. For the first time in weeks, he felt a bit hopeful. Then he smiled to himself at how similar he and Pederson were – like kindred spirits. Slowly, blackness and silence descended.

A nudging woke him some time later.

"It's safe to go now."

Dad roused Pederson, then pushed the snowmobile out of the entrance and warmed the motor as Daniel gathered their belongings and doused the fire. Pederson stirred, but when he tried to walk he was hunched over and stiff-legged. He collapsed back down on his bedding, wheezing and coughing. Daniel and his dad slid him out through the snow-encrusted entrance on the sleeping bag, then gently lifted him onto the Ski-Doo.

The frosty glitter of sunshine made them squint, but once their eyes had adjusted, they set off. The dogs scampered ahead with Dactyl in the lead. They cut through the huge drifts of snow, leaving a wavering pathway behind them.

Mom took one look at Pederson and insisted he be taken straight to the hospital for a checkup. He didn't have a chance to resist. He was lying in a hospital bed within the hour, being rehydrated and treated for bronchitis.

Although he insisted on being released the next day, he was only given permission on the condition that he return to the Bringham home, where Daniel's mom could take care of him. So, armed with a prescription for antibiotics and an inhaler, plus strict instructions to have plenty of fluids and rest, Pederson came to stay.

CHAPTER TWELVE

The kids on the bus surrounded Daniel the next morning. As usual Jed had spilled the news almost as soon as Daniel had filled him in about his adventures. He'd called Jed right after the blizzard to tell him about their narrow escape. First, his friend had opened his mouth and told his chatty sisters that Pederson was staying at Daniel's house, and then his parents. They'd somehow spread it from there. Now the whole town seemed to know.

Squishing himself onto the back seat of the bus between Jed and some of the other boys, Daniel gave his friend a poke in the shoulder and said, "See, can't tell you anything!"

When he saw Jed's obvious embarrassment, Daniel grinned.

"Doesn't matter now." He poked Jed again and then whispered a warning. "Everyone knows about Pederson staying at my place, but don't you dare breathe a word about where my hideout is, or my plans for a research place, or I'll never tell you anything again!"

Jed gulped.

"Don't tell me you've told already?"

Jed shook his head emphatically. "I swear, I didn't. I'll try not to say anything else," he said, squirming on his seat.

Daniel was glad he hadn't told Jed the full details about Pederson's Edmontosaurus find. They were trying to keep it quiet until the museum people came and Pederson was fully recovered from his bout of bronchitis.

Brett swaggered to the back of the bus and prodded Daniel. "So you have a murderer staying with you," he said loudly.

All of a sudden the noise on the bus stopped and everyone turned to look at Daniel.

Jed grinned and Daniel laughed. "He didn't murder anyone."

"Yeah, right!" said Wade, joining them. "What about those bones he was hacking up on his table?"

"Skeletal bones from archaeological digs," Daniel said somewhat smugly, keeping the main news to himself. "He's a paleontologist."

"You were really in his place?" asked Craig, the braver of the Nelwin twins, with his big eyes turned intently on Daniel.

"What was it like?" Lucy, one of Jed's sisters, asked, squeezing herself in beside Daniel.

"Yes, I've been there a couple of times," he answered. "It was no big deal. He sort of camps out in his cabin, with only a few pieces of furniture and a wood stove. He's just a scientist, who lives on his own."

" 'Cause he murdered his wife!" Brett interjected.

Daniel sighed. "No, he didn't."

"I saw the cross," piped up Wade.

"I think that's just where he found some other fossils."

"Well, what about all those jars of poison, then?" asked Brett.

"Harmless! Just teas, and herbs, and cooking stuff," Daniel said patiently. "I ought to know. I made tea for him when he got sick."

"Weren't you scared going there?" Lucy asked quietly. Her sisters Lindsay and Leanne moved in to stand tightly beside her, their eyes big and round with anxious curiosity.

Daniel nodded. "I was at first. He has a huge dog! It's called Bear – and it looks like one!"

Then he launched into the story of when he had first met Pederson, leaving out the fact that he had been in his secret hideout at the time. The kids on the bus were all hanging off the edges of their seats to listen.

O ver the next few days, Daniel spent as much time as he could with Pederson. He seemed shy and reluctant to say much at first, especially to Daniel's parents, but one day Daniel came home from school to find him chatting with Dad.

As usual, the vaporizer sent swirls of mist into the air. Sunlight filtered through the sheers, giving a warm glow to the pale blue room. An antique maple dresser stood opposite the foot of the bed, under a large oval portrait of Daniel's great-grandparents.

"You were right, Ole. I talked to the bank manager again, as you suggested," Dad said, shifting uncomfortably on a straight-backed wooden chair that he'd pulled up to the bedside.

He continued, "There may be something we can do yet. When I told them that the experts from the Royal Saskatchewan Museum and the Royal Tyrrell Museum were coming to take a look, they seemed willing to give me a little more time to sort things out." Then Dad raised his shoulders in a gesture of awe. "They want to talk to the people you contacted."

"I'll give you their names," Pederson said, coughing slightly.

"I'd appreciate that."

"I'm glad to hear my past experience has come to some use." Pederson sighed. "I'm a little surprised they gave me the time of day, to tell you the truth. Haven't been in touch with anyone in Drumheller or Regina since my wife died. I'd guess half of them have never heard of me."

Daniel moved to stand beside Dad, sliding his backpack to the floor with a small thud. "Yes, they have – I saw all those articles with your name on them in those magazines."

"Magazines?"

"The ones I left on your table." Daniel felt his face flush again at his failure to return the books to the shelves. *"Palaeontographica Canadiana,* or something like that."

"You mean the journals."

Daniel nodded.

Dad stared at Pederson in wonder. "You've done write-ups in professional journals? I'm impressed," he said.

"That was a few years back when I was still working in the regular paleontology circles. Then I became fed up and branched out on my own." Pederson sighed again and stared at the ceiling, deep in thought.

Daniel noticed how frail Pederson looked. He was lying in the double bed under the puffy quilt with a blanket stacked on top. His grey hair was combed and flat on his head. Even his beard was combed down. But his eyes still held some sadness.

""Well, I'd best get back to my chores," Dad said, standing up. As he headed for the door, he nodded pointedly in Daniel's direction. "We'll see you shortly."

"I'll be right there, Dad," he promised. "Mr. Pederson, do you want to rest now, or would you like to see a new book on dinosaurs I just found in the school library?"

A glint of interest sparked in the old man's eyes, and Daniel grabbed his backpack and dug out the book. He handed it over, propping a pillow behind it so that it wouldn't flop out of his hands.

"Here let me fix the pillows behind you so you can read." Daniel adjusted them behind Pederson's back.

"I'll be back in a while," he said, smiling and heading to the door.

"Ah, Daniel?" said Pederson. "Would you mind finding my glasses before you go?"

Daniel looked at Pederson in surprise. "Your glasses?"

"Yes, I wear glasses, and your mother tucked them away somewhere. I'm supposed to use them all the time, but I can't be bothered," he admitted shyly.

Daniel checked the night table by the bed, and found them in the top drawer. He opened the case carefully and handed them to Pederson, who smiled his thanks. He raised the book to start reading, as Daniel left the room.

A few days later, Daniel noticed Pederson's coughing didn't seem as harsh, and the colour of his face looked a more healthy pink. His speech came out more evenly and normal, and there wasn't any more rattling in his chest when he breathed. Daniel was happy he was improving, but it also meant he'd be leaving soon.

When Pederson did go home a week later, Daniel was sorry to see him leave, but knew he'd see him again soon.

Pederson had invited him to assist with the Edmontosaurus dig whenever he had time after his chores and school. Daniel was really getting to know the old guy. It was great to finally have someone to share his interest in dinosaurs. Someone with a real dinosaur in his backyard!

A couple of weeks passed. A few days before Christmas, Daniel's dad knocked on his bedroom door. As usual Daniel was pouring over a dinosaur book, but he jumped up when Dad entered quickly, carrying a large plastic bag from the Co-op store.

"Hi, Son," Dad said, peering around. He set the bag on the floor by the door, then came hesitantly over to the desk and looked at Daniel's book. *"Dinosaurs of the Prairies,"* he read. "Is there anything in there about the Edmontosaurus?" he asked.

Daniel grinned. "Sure. They were one of the first duckbills discovered in Alberta. There just weren't any intact skeletons until now."

Dad fingered the dinosaur replicas on the shelf, and then caught sight of the receptaculites fossil on Daniel's dresser. "How did you know what that was?"

"I've been studying the books for a long time. Then last year, when our class went to Eastend, I bought a book put out by the Royal Saskatchewan Museum that had the taculite it in. When I came across the rock, I put two and two together."

"You sure seem to understand paleontology," Dad smiled. "You don't get it from me, so it must come from your mother's side of the family. All I know about is farming and ranching."

"That's all related to geology," said Daniel earnestly, "and it's an important aspect, too."

Dad tousled Daniel's hair and sat on the edge of the bed. Then he pointed to the bag by the door.

"What's this?" Daniel asked, going over and opening it up. He pulled out a thick grey woollen blanket. Something hard was wrapped inside. Carefully, he unfolded it. A camping lantern? He looked up at Dad in surprise.

"They're for your hideout," Dad said, and smiled. "Just in case you ever get storm-stayed again, which I hope you never do!"

"Thanks, Dad! This is great!" Daniel felt a glow of pleasure.

"Seriously, Son, I figured you could make use of them while you're on your digs," he grinned shyly. "I have something important to tell you, too."

He smiled up at Daniel, then said, "We've done it. Mr. Pederson's contacts convinced the bank that there were some viable archaeological finds around here. On the strength of that, the manager is willing to take the pressure off for awhile, and may even consider giving us an extension."

"Wahoo!!" Daniel threw his arms into the air, holding the blanket and the lantern, and then danced in a little circle.

"Now don't get too excited," Dad warned. "Our land

isn't totally saved. We still have to look into various options for income and figure out how to come up with the payments."

"But, remember what Mr. Pederson said, Dad?" Daniel felt a quiver of anticipation. "The dinosaur finds could be turned into an income."

"Yes, but I'm not clear exactly how that works. But I do know that it could take quite a while before anything happens. Apparently it takes as much finagling to fund scientists as it does farmers." Dad ruffled Daniel's hair again.

"Great!" Daniel smiled. "I knew there had to be a way."

"You sure did, but don't count on it yet. We don't know what will happen." Dad stood up and walked over to the door.

"I know, but at least we can check it out."

Dad stroked his chin. "We'll look into things in the new year. In the meantime, I can keep farming."

With a nod, he left the room.

Pederson was the last to arrive for Christmas dinner. Daniel greeted him at the back door. By the time he'd removed his boots and overcoat, his new bifocal glasses were fogged up – the air was moist from the pots of vegetables cooking. As he led him into the dining room, Daniel noticed how important Pederson looked with his clean-shaven face, and dressed in clean pants and a shirt with a tie.

Pederson stopped to look at the festive room, which was decorated with silver garlands along the walls and doorways. A huge red crepe bell hung from the middle of the ceiling light fixture. A six-foot blue spruce Christmas tree stood between the dining room and the living room, with lights that twinkled on and off, and a huge glittery star on top.

The tree ornaments were a colourful mix of old-fashioned sparklers and newer satin balls, crocheted snowflakes, small handmade wooden toys, and candy canes. Some of the decorations had once belonged to Daniel's relatives, some were new things his family had acquired over the years. There were even the construction paper ones he'd made in school. More silver garlands finished off the tree.

The dining room was warm and cozy, with a bright white-and-red Christmas tablecloth on the table and a small potted poinsettia in the centre, courtesy of Jed's parents. The table was set with Daniel's grandmother's best china, along with matching burgundy napkins. The good dishes were only used for special occasions like Christmas and Easter. Already the tossed salad, cranberry sauce, cold ham, and buns were on the table.

Daniel introduced Pederson to the Lindstrom family, scattered about the room. Doug Lindstrom, Jed's dad, patted him on the back and stood chatting with him, while Jed's cheerful mom, Greta, placed a huge platter of turkey on the table, then waved from across the room.

Lucy, Lindsay, and Leanne entered, carrying bowls of vegetables, cabbage rolls, and dressing to the table, and then they took their places. When they were introduced, they giggled and hid their faces, a little in awe of the hermit they'd heard so much about. Pederson nodded shyly at everyone as they took their seats.

Daniel's dad greeted Pederson like an old friend, shaking his hand before he took his place at the head of the table. Daniel grinned over at Jed, who studied the old man carefully. Jed's three sisters pulled their chairs closer together and stared at Pederson openly, trying to determine if he was someone to be wary of or not. When Cheryl gurgled and cooed at him from her highchair and he winked at her, they all relaxed.

Once everyone was seated, Mom came in and set the bowl of steaming hot gravy down on the table. As she took her place, everyone complimented her over her preparation of the meal. It did look spectacular.

Dad poured wine for the adults and Mom made sure all the kids had juice. Then Dad rose with his glass in his hand.

"I'd like to start off by making a toast to Ole Pederson." He raised his glass. "First of all, thank you for saving our son!"

Pederson nodded his head slightly.

Then Daniel's dad continued. "And secondly, even though we've still got some figuring out to do, we couldn't have kept the farm intact without you," Dad toasted, tipping his glass in their new friend's direction. "To Ole Pederson, a lifesaver in more ways than one."

Pederson sat beaming modestly, as everyone clinked their glasses and sipped. Daniel was surprised when he shuffled to his feet a few moments later.

"Thank you, but, ah, I'd also like to propose a toast...to young Daniel, here," he said, raising his glass in the air. "Without him, I wouldn't have come to know you good people. Come to think of it, he's also responsible for saving my life at least twice."

Pederson bent and nudged Daniel in the shoulder. "Did you ever think about becoming a doctor, lad?"

Daniel could feel his face burning, but only smiled as everyone raised their glasses to him. Then the laughing and talking resumed as they began passing the food around the table. Everyone ate heartily and by the time Mom presented the choice of Saskatoon pie, shortbread cookies, or mince tarts for dessert, Daniel was too full to have anything. He also knew Mom had Nanaimo bars, sugar cookies, and butter tarts for coffee later. He and Jed clutched their stomachs and groaned.

A few moments later, Pederson seemed fidgety, and then he stood up again and spoke quietly.

"Ah. I'd like to say thank you to all of you for taking care of me so well, and being so kind," he smiled and raised his glass of wine at Daniel and his parents. "What I'd like to do, that is, I'd like to say..." He looked around in bewilderment at the table full of expectant, smiling faces.

Then he focused on Daniel's dad and continued, "What I mean to do is, ah, well, although I can't lease out my land, because I promised my wife before she died a couple of years ago that I would never do that. She believed in my dreams, you see."

Pederson's face flushed a bright red, and he pushed his glasses back into place as everyone sat quietly, waiting for him to go on.

"Well what I'm trying to say is that I'd like to offer you Bringham folks a short-term interest-free loan. Mind it would only be until we get our joint venture going. But I happen to have a bit put aside, and I can't think of a better use for it than sharing it with my good neighbours here."

Daniel's parents glanced at each other in amazement.

"Wow," said Daniel, jumping up from the dinner table. "Do you really mean it? Dad, does that mean we can stay here for sure and I can keep Gypsy?"

"Whoa, wait a minute Son, calm down," said Dad. He turned to Pederson. "I can't let you do that."

"Why in tarnation not?" Pederson seemed surprised. "Besides, I have a stake in seeing that your land isn't torn up, too. You never know what might be hidden here."

Dad was astounded at first. Then he looked at Mom, and she shrugged back. "Are you sure about this, Mr. Pederson?"

Pederson said, proudly. "I'm sure. Since young Daniel first came to pay me that unexpected visit, my life hasn't been so lonely. Besides, now there's an opportunity to do what I've always wanted."

Daniel had never seen his parents so speechless. They sat humbly, with their eyes shining.

Sitting back down, Pederson stared down at his plate for a few moments, then continued to speak in a soft voice. "When the museum board wouldn't give me a leave of absence or funding to prove my theories, I decided to go my own way. I took early retirement and moved up here."

"The fact is," Pederson went on, "Now that I've proved my point, I've been thinking about getting myself a place in town, at least when I'm not working at the excavation site. My health isn't what it used to be." He winked at Daniel. "If I do that, I'll need someone to watch the place here for me. We could maybe figure it out as some sort of payment in kind."

Daniel and Jed exchanged significant looks. This could make for some great weekend adventures.

"Say, yes, Dad, Mom," Daniel implored, as he looked at his parents' surprised faces.

They nodded in agreement with broad smiles.

"Okay," Dad told Pederson. Then he laughed and said to Daniel, "I guess I could learn to take your advice once in a while."

Daniel looked over joyfully at Pederson. Jed gave him the thumbs-up. The Lindstroms cheered and complimented Pederson, who sat quietly contented. When

Daniel's mom got up and gave him a hug, two bright red spots of embarrassment appeared on his cheeks. Daniel grinned.

A tinkling spoon tapping against a wine glass drew everyone's attention to Greta Lindstrom. "While we're on the subject of the partnership and the dinosaur research," she said, "I'll let you in on a little secret. Just between us."

Daniel looked over at Jed. Now he knew why Jed could never keep a secret – the trait came from his mother.

"As you know, I work part-time in the town council office. I happen to know that the bank manager has already talked to the mayor," she said with pleasure. "They figure the finds would be a great boon to the town's economy in terms of tourists coming to visit the area, which I know you all hope will happen, too. Well," she revealed, "They're planning to invite you to go to the next town council meeting in January to talk about the possibilities. They want to get involved and help."

Everyone clapped at this news!

Daniel turned eagerly to his dad. "And I bet there are some government departments, and scientists, and maybe even archaeological societies and museums that would give us advice on how to set up this kind of thing!"

Pederson patted Daniel enthusiastically on the back. Daniel flushed.

"I have some other contacts who might be willing to help with that aspect, too," added Pederson. "We'll see it's done properly."

Then Doug Lindstrom piped up, "We'd like to help in any way we can, as well." Greta and Jed nodded in agreement. The girls nodded solemnly too, but didn't seem quite sure about what was going on.

Daniel jumped up and raised his juice glass. "To great partnerships and great friends!" He beamed at Pederson. "And to even greater dinosaur finds!"

EPILOGUE

A year and a half later, Daniel stood beside Pederson at the opening of their new town museum. The town council had voted unanimously to donate the old rink for a small museum and research station. Plans for the future included a new fully equipped building, but that would take some time and fundraising. In the meantime, they'd established an impressive collection. The temporary centre was already attracting tourists and paleontology buffs.

Daniel's family had survived their financial crunch with the help of Pederson and the loan extensions from the bank. They were still operating the farm, although on a smaller scale. They spent a lot of their time now constructing their own tourist attraction, with hiking trails and sites for overnight camping excavations. Jed's dad had gone away to work in Regina for a while to save their farm. The Lindstroms had also partnered with the Bringhams and Pederson. They planned to help run the tourist booth, refreshment area, group tour bookings and, once things swung into full gear, transporting people out to the digs.

Pederson concentrated on the actual excavations, supervising the teams that came out from the museums and universities. Daniel was his primary assistant on the weekends. Jed often appeared as well, but Pederson and Daniel never told him any really confidential information until they were ready for everyone to know.

Today, Pederson, with a museum staff badge pinned to his shirt, pointed to a display that showed an assemblage of dinosaur bones and a replica of a nest with Edmontosaurus eggs. Paleontology experts at the Royal Saskatchewan Museum in Regina, along with several from the Royal Tyrrell Museum in Drumheller, were still studying the real ones, especially the baby skeleton. The skull had been studied and released for display.

The full-scale Edmontosaurus that Pederson had unearthed had been assembled and erected nearby in a huge roped-off area. It stood about two and a half metres high, with a series of bumps running along its neck, back, and tail. Its hind legs were larger than the front ones, and its protruding jaw contained hundreds of teeth. Exhibits along the walls showed stages of geological evolution, then excavation phases, and samples of fossils found in the region. Huge drawings and posters depicted the creatures of the Cretaceous period found in the province so far.

The room was jammed. A group of Daniel's schoolmates surrounded him and Pederson. At the back of the crowd, a handful of parents, including Daniel's and Jed's, stood with photographers and newspaper reporters from the local paper and all over the province. One Regina television crew, another from Swift Current, and a third from Medicine Hat were also taping the grand opening of the centre.

Daniel felt his heart expanding as Pederson explained the exhibit. "This is also the first hadrosaur-type skull to be discovered," he said proudly, pointing to the skull.

Then he explained, "The hadrosaur was the first American dinosaur to be described, and the first nearly complete skeleton found. It was discovered in 1858 in New Jersey in the United States, but it was skull-less, although hundreds of teeth were found."

Pederson guided them over to a highlighted display of a replicated nest with the baby skeleton.

"And so, you see, the Edmontosauruses appear to have been highly social creatures. They probably travelled in herds and seem to have laid eggs in communal nests. That means that several females dropped their eggs in the same nests."

He directed them to take a closer look at the diorama of his dig, where he described how he had located the nest.

"This is the first conclusive evidence of nests and eggs of this particular species," he said, "although there have been a couple of other types of hadrosaurs found elsewhere in North America – in Alberta and Montana to be precise."

The group of students broke out into excited conversation.

"Mr. Pederson, doesn't that mean that the information in most museums will have to be updated?" Jed asked loudly over the noisy crowd.

"Yes, it does, young man," Pederson nodded. "New discoveries are always challenging our assumptions in the world of paleontology."

"And this also means the books have to be rewritten," Daniel spoke up.

"Indeed it does, Daniel. So others can say they 'saw it in a book' too." Pederson winked at him.

Daniel's parents had moved up beside him. He felt Dad's arm squeeze his shoulder, and Mom gave him a hug. He gazed out over the crowd of classmates and noticed Brett and Wade staring attentively and in respectful awe of Pederson. About time – calling him a murderer!

"There are many more explorations to conduct, and we don't know what else may be out there," Pederson said. "It takes a great deal of enthusiasm and dedication, like young Daniel here has, to unearth these irreplaceable relics of an extinct species." Pederson smiled at him. "And I'm sure he'll make some great discoveries of his own someday."

Daniel smiled and squeezed the lucky receptaculites

fossil in his pocket. He hadn't turned it in to be put on display. It was private. In fact, he still had a few interesting stones stashed in his secret hideout. And *that* was definitely going to stay off limits!

BIBLIOGRAPHY

Reid, Monty, *The Last Great Dinosaurs: An illustrated Guide to Alberta's Dinosaurs,* Red Deer College Press, Red Deer, Alberta, 1990, ISBN: 0-88995-055-5.

Stewart, Janet, *The Dinosaurs: A New Discovery,* Hayes Publishing Ltd., Burlington, Ontario, 1989, ISBN: 0-88625-235-0.

Storer, Dr. John, *Geological History of Saskatchewan,* Saskatchewan Museum of Natural History, Government of Saskatchewan, 1989.

Wallace, Joseph, *The Rise and Fall of the Dinosaur,* Michael Friedman Publishing Group, Inc., New York, N.Y., 1987, ISBN:0-8317-2368-8.

URL: http://www.enchantedlearning.com

VOCABULARY/DESCRIPTIONS

The paleontological material found throughout this novel comes mostly from the Cretaceous period. A brief description of some of the terms used follows, with their pronunciations. The Frenchman Valley, where this story takes place, is located in the southwest and central areas of Saskatchewan.

COPROLITE: *(KOWP-ruh-lyte)* ("dung stone"):
Coprolite is fossilized feces (animal waste). The term coprolite was coined around 1830, when the earliest-known specimens were found. They are quite common now.

CRETACEOUS PERIOD *(cree–TAY-shush):*
The Cretaceous period lasted from about 146 to 65 million years ago. Flowering plants and trees made their first widespread appearance, creating bright beautiful land-

scapes with their reds, yellows, and purples. Before that time, the browns and greens of trees and ferns were contrasted only by the blues of the skies and seas. The Cretaceous period was the latter part of the Mesozoic era, when great creatures roamed the land and pterosaurs, huge flying creatures, ruled the skies. A variety of small creatures also populated the earth and seas. The climate was tropical all year round.

NOTE: *Creta is the Latin word for chalk. The Cretaceous period is named for chalky rock from southeastern England that was the first Cretaceous period sediment studied.*

CRINOIDS *(crin-OIDS):*
A lily-shaped or star-shaped marine animal, usually sedentary with feathery arms.

EDMONTOSAURUS *(ed-MON-toh-SAWR-us):*
A large plant-eating member of the duckbill dinosaurs, or hadrosaurs, that lived from about 73 to 65 million years ago during the Cretaceous period in western North America. With 800 to 1600 teeth crowded together along the side of the huge jaws, they were able to eat tough leaves and other vegetation. This flat-headed duckbill grew to 13 metres (42 feet) long, 3 metres (9 feet) tall at the hips, and weighed from 3200 to 3600 kilograms (7000 to 8000 pounds). Edmontosaurus was a slow-moving dinosaur with few defences, but its keen senses may have helped it to avoid predators in its swampy habitat.

HADROSAUR *(HAD-roh-SAWR)* ("bulky lizard"):
The hadrosaurs were a group of duck-billed dinosaurs that ranged in size from 3 to 12 metres (10 to 40 feet) long and lived in the late Cretaceous period. They appear to have been highly social creatures, laying eggs in nests communally, travelling and even migrating in herds. Similar in body-build, the main difference between hadrosaur species was in the shape and size of the crest on their heads. In Alberta alone, remains from twelve different hadrosaur species have been discovered. Nests with eggs have been found in both Alberta and Montana.

MOSASAUR *(MOES-ah-SAWR):*
Mosasaurs were giant, snakelike marine reptiles that extended from 12.5 to 17.6 metres (40 to 59 feet) long. They were not dinosaurs, but were related to snakes and monitor lizards. Powerful swimmers, mosasaurs had adapted to living in shallow seas, and breathed air. These carnivores were a short-lived line of reptiles that went extinct during the K-T extinction, some 65 million years ago.

PALEONTOLOGY *(PAY-lee-on-TALL-o-gee):*
Paleontology is the branch of geology that deals with prehistoric forms of life through the study of plant and animal fossils.

PTERODACTYLS *(ter-oh-DAK-tils)* ("winged finger"):
Pterodactyls were flying prehistoric reptiles of the pterosaur family. They had wingspans that spread up to 6 metres (20 feet), made up of skin stretched along the body between the hind limb and a very long fourth digit of the forelimb.

RECEPTACULITES *(ree-sep-TACK-you-light-EEZE):*
Referred to as the "sunflower coral" from 450 million years ago. At one time, it was thought to be a sponge. In more recent times, receptaculites are considered to be sponge-like, rather than true sponges. They are commonly found as flattened stones with a pattern of criss-cross lines like the head of a ripe sunflower.

SPONGES:
Also called poriferans, sponges are very simple animals that live permanently attached to one location in the water. There are from 5,000 to 10,000 known species. Most sponges live in salt water – only about 150 species thrive in fresh water. Sponges evolved over 500 million years ago.

STROMATOLITES *(strow- MAT-o-LIGHT-ees):*
Mounds built up of layers of green algae and trapped sediment.

TYRANNOSAURUS REX (tie-RAN-o-SAWR-us rex):
The tyrannosaurus rex is also known as the "Tyrant lizard king". A carnivore (meat-eater) that ate large dinosaurs like the triceratops, it was 12.4 metres (40 feet) long, 4.6 to 6 metres (15 to 20 feet) tall, and weighed 5 to 7 tonnes. It lived during the late Cretaceous period, from about 85 to 65 million years ago. Tyrannosaurus rex's arms were only about 1 metre (3 feet) long, and it had two-fingered hands. T-rex had cone-shaped, serrated teeth that were continually replaced. The first Tyrannosaurus rex fossil was discovered by the famous fossil hunter Barnum Brown in 1902. Only about 30 Tyrannosaurus fossils have been found, mostly in the western part of the United States. The Tyrannosaurus rex skeleton in Saskatchewan was found in 1994, at Eastend, and was excavated by the Royal Saskatchewan Museum.

ROYAL SASKATCHEWAN MUSEUM FOSSIL RESEARCH STATION:
In 1994, the RSM began the excavation of what was then only the thirteenth-known partial skeleton of the carnivorous dinosaur Tyrannosaurus rex, now affectionately called Scotty. This project led to the establishment of a fossil research station in Eastend in 1995. The RSM's activities there focus on paleontological field research and collecting, the separation of fossils from their rock matrix in the laboratory, and ongoing research to better understand Saskatchewan's fossil history.

ACKNOWLEDGEMENTS:

Special thanks to Alison Lohans for helping me achieve the life of the story, and to Dianne Warren who saw the potential. I am most grateful to my editor, Joanne Gerber, for her insights that enriched the essence, and without whose skill this book would not have reached its present form.

Thanks also to: Ervin Fehr for the initial idea and inspiration; Harold Bryant, Curator of Earth Sciences, Royal Saskatchewan Museum, for his expert advice; The Children's Writers Round Robin group in Saskatchewan for their encouragement; Linda McDowell for first taking me to the T-rex excavation site; and others along the way who have influenced, inspired, and informed.

NB: The paleontological information in this book has been derived from a wide variety of written and pictorial sources. Although I have done my best to create an accurate picture, this remains a work of fiction, and there is no claim to total academic authenticity. New discoveries constantly change what scientists know about the world of dinosaurs.

ABOUT THE AUTHOR

J UDITH SILVERTHORNE is the author of two books, including a juvenile novel *The Secret of Sentinel Rock* for which she won the 1996 Saskatchewan Book Award for Children's Literature. She has also worked as an editor, curator, and a television documentary producer, as well as serving as the Executive Director for the Saskatchewan Library Association. She currently lives in Regina.

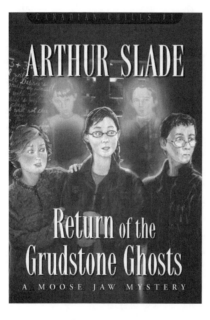